Also by JOSHUA SENTER
Daisies

STILL THE NIGHT CALL

STILL THE NIGHT CALL

JOSHUA SENTER

www.RoubidouxPress.com

Roubidoux Press
www.RoubidouxPress.com

First published in January 2022 by Roubidoux Press.

ISBN #978-1-7375856-0-2
eISBN #978-1-7375856-1-9

National Suicide Prevention Lifeline
#800-273-8255

*It is as painful perhaps to be awakened
from a vision as to be born.*

- James Joyce

To my love, my life, my favorite thing-my Jesse.
With you, I know I am not alone.

THE NIGHT CALL

*E*veryone knows the story of the ruthless serpent that slithers into the garden, that lays waste to Eden, that changes the fate of mankind forever. In the beginning, it slides along so silent and careful you don't even know it's there in the dark with you curled up under your pillow. If it rouses you from sleep, at first you may simply turn on a fan to numb the sound of its hiss or add another blanket to your bed to warm the cold patches where its skin chills yours. Later on, when you become unnerved by its presence, you'll drink some warm milk to ease your mind or down some strong whiskey to crawl back into the berth where you know it waits. But pop a pill or shoot some heroin, nothing can stop it from telling you all the things you don't want to hear. It lingers in the inky silence of wherever you may find to close your eyes because it craves the dark most, where its words can't easily be ignored, where it can tear through every fortification of peace and quiet you may try and put up. And of course, your ears perk to the slightest utterance of its all too familiar voice. Then from the tiniest crack it makes in your mind, it expands out like a virus intertwining fact and fiction until they become a mutated gospel of the world around you and your place in it. And that is the real depravity of it—the snake, the Night Call—how you can work to silence it, to split it up into what's real and what isn't, but it doesn't matter what you tell yourself, it can overrule those words, jumble them up and make them gibberish, make you short of breath, make your heart race, make you sweat, make you bleed. It refuses to let you go peacefully into the land of your dreams.

You know what I'm talking about, don't you? You've lain twisted in your sheets, choking for air, arguing with the Night Call, begging it to get off your chest and out of your ear, to let you sleep. But it will not relent. It enjoys the torture. Evening after evening, it arrives, zealous for attention, with a laundry list of all your shortcomings. *You have failed not just yourself*, it whispers, *you have failed everyone else too. You aren't worthy of the light in your eyes, your existence is of no value, you are dead weight—a worthless anchor broken off from any meaningful foundation. You are a mistake, accidentally born into this world for no reason other than for nature to test the powers of the pain it can exact on a nothing before a nothing chooses to be even more of a nothing. Father, you have not provided for your family. Husband, you are inadequate. Mother, you have not raised your children well. Wife, you are a fool. Sister, you are not worthy of praise. Brother, you have not brought us the hope of tomorrow. Everyone and everything beautiful is turned against you.*

The clock ticks on minute by infuriating minute reminding you how long you've been tormented. One hour turns into two, two hours into four. You will soon get up to start your day exhausted from the Night Call's evil tidings. But even the light will become like the dark. Everything will blur together, reality and dreams, truth and falsehoods. Like acid poured over the two hemispheres of your cerebrum, it disrupts the chemicals that balance your thoughts, burning through your pleasure and pain receptors until you can no longer distinguish one from the other. This is its plan, to seep into your hindbrain, cut off your oxygen and leave your stomach full of bile that eats you from the inside. You will not even recognize your face, the hollow eyes, the despondent lips, the ashen skin. People will ask if there is something wrong, but what can you tell them, that you're lost, that you've been lead astray by a demon, dashed against the rocks, and now wait for it to claim your soul from your lifeless flesh? You tell yourself you are the only one incapable of tuning it out. Others hear the Night Call but can justify their existence. You cannot.

"Your honor, I have not lived up to my potential," you hear yourself cry. "Indeed, I should have done things differently. I should have done things like everyone else. I should have led a perfect life. Surely there was a flawless existence in store for me, every right move laid out. All I needed to do was pluck those choices up into a smiling bouquet of magnificence, but I have not. I have gathered weeds and worms and gnats and grubs, *and worthless now, I stand before the everlasting image of who I could have been. But I am not that person. I will never be that person. The mirror is broken and cannot be fixed. The shards of potential have splintered into an infinity of ineptitude I can no longer bear to look at. It hurts my eyes—all five trillion of them staring back at me, blinking like razor blades, tearing through my soul. So damn me, I beg you. Pass judgement upon me. I know I will not receive heaven, but even hell would be better than this purgatory in which I find myself now."*

Here is the verdict: You are guilty—guilty of it all! The goal you missed. The move you didn't make. The lies you can't take back. The hurt you can't fix. The job you lost. The career you'll never have. The baby you failed. The animal you neglected. The house you burnt down. The city you destroyed. You asshole! You fucker! You have the wrong color skin and the wrong sex and the wrong soul. You've been born at the wrong time in the wrong country on the wrong planet. And all this you could have changed, all this you could have done differently. This is what the Night Call assures you, even if you try to believe it's not true—even if it's not true. Across the universe of time and space, it flutters like a moth on wings made of the ashes of the dead, proclaiming as long as there is more, there will always be less. And you, you are that less. You are less than less. And you will always be less until you are nothing.

Slowly, the Night Call chokes you like a vengeful lover, constricting until it snaps your head from your body the moment you stop fighting it. And you do want to stop fighting. After all of this, you want to give it everything it desires, every nook and cranny, every molecule and atom and quark shooting across the galaxies—everywhere and nowhere. You yearn to disappear into nothingness without mass or form or meaning so it can't reach you any longer. Still, it doesn't seem to know it has broken you, that you are not coming back. The pieces are on the floor shattered, and there is no one to paste them together anymore, no tender hand to reverse this course. Doesn't it see that? Doesn't it understand it has won? So why even now in your last hours, does it torment you? Especially now in your final breaths, it brutalizes your mind with the unforgiving blows of its poisonous fangs as though you're not on your belly already, spine ripped out of you, slick in your own blood. Unless...

Unless there's something it's not letting on, some hope yet able to pierce its venom now choking out your existence. Is it right there in front of you, just to your left or right? Will salvation somehow make itself known before the Night Call does you in? Is that what it's scared of, that there's another possibility, other than death, as long as your lungs still pull oxygen? Is that why it's on top of you, putrid breath in your face, holding you down, twisting in the screws, because there's still...hope?

4:30AM

This is going to be the last day of my life. I know this when I wake up, how it will end. This is what it's all been building up to. This blessed day. Despite the itch in the back of my mind knowing what's to come, I do what I do every morning and get out of bed. I don't stretch over the mattress. I don't yawn. I refuse to be a sloth. I can't hear the siren's call of the warm sheets. I became deaf to it years ago. I am alone. The house is freezing. The late October chill of a Southern Missouri fall easily bombards the thin farmhouse walls around me. Even still, I take a cold shower to wake up. It don't hurt standing under a stream of ice. I'm used to it by now. It makes me keen, tells my body to prepare for the day ahead. There will be no rest for you, Calem Dewayne Honeycutt.

I shave because I have to. I'm hairy all over just like my pop and his pop before him, and being clean-shaven means you're a gentleman according to my mom. All this hair is because—also according to her—we're Irish. Dark, black Irish. I looked up Ireland one time on a map. All I know is it's fucking far from this place.

Dixie, my ol' hound dog is sleeping next to the kitchen door as I dress and fix the coffee pot. While I pour food into her bowl, I run through the list of what needs done this morning: milk the cows, help Pop string up new barbwire down by the crick, take that trailer full of walnuts over to Kell's, swing by InterCounty Bank to pay my mortgage. Suddenly, I stop. I clench my stomach, double over in pain. Shit.

Dixie helps herself to breakfast while I eat a half-dozen antacid tablets and wash 'em down with a cup of Folgers. I stare out at the bruised hue of the morning sky trying to forget the pain in my gut. Doctor says I need to stop drinking coffee. I should try tea instead. Guess I could guzzle Mountain Dew like my best friend Miles, but I'd probably gain two-hundred pounds like he did too.

Just as the last stars in the sky begin to vanish, I grab a handful of the jerky I dried from the backstrap of an eight-point buck I shot last fall, throw a cap on my head, and exit the house without locking up. If anybody bothers to come this far out—a good twenty minutes from town off Z Highway—they can have whatever they find. Besides, the only real thing of value we got out here you can't easily steal: hills and hollers choked full of alfalfa and oak trees and Holsteins—seventy-nine last count.

Pop is already in the milk barn when I arrive, and that makes me feel like shit. His hips is bad and his knees are worse. The way his knuckles have swelled up like ticks over the last few years don't help neither. I always try to be the one to turn on the lights, even though I know he don't like that. He don't like being advanced in his years. I don't blame him. I hate being thirty-two. I'm too old to not know better and too young to know enough. We don't say a word when we see each other—him checking a hose in the milking stage that might've been leaking yesterday—but he knows I'm here. I grab a gas jug to fill the four-wheelers so we can bring up the cows.

The girls are all standing around waiting in the bottom of the back forty when Pop and I arrive on our four-wheelers to lead 'em up to the barn. They know us, can tell us apart. And I know each one of them, every spot—black *and* white. I know when they're tired or in pain or feeling good. They're my babies. I've even named a few of 'em. Frieda reminds me of the gossipy postmaster in town, always chewing her cud and making trouble. Mandy is named after my high school girlfriend. She's one of the prettiest heifers I've ever seen, dark face with a clean white collar 'round her neck and a trim body that sways when she walks. Donna is the fattest cow we have. Bert is the ugliest. The rest of 'em fall somewhere in between, and I've probably given 'em all a name here or there like Burger, Steak, Prime Rib, or Fuck You.

They don't need encouraging. Once I open the gate, they follow Pop up the hill to the milk barn. Bert is always at the front, and Frieda is always at the tail end. After Frieda is through the gate, I close it back up and hop on my idling four-wheeler to trail after 'em, making sure no one decides to cut loose from the rest of the herd and wander off. Not that they would. They wait for their milkings, morning and evening, wanting to get rid of the heavy cream in their udders something awful. I know some folks say it's unnatural for us to milk cows, that they ain't happy about it or some crazy notion, but those folks ain't ever been to a milk barn or met a real Holstein happy to have a purpose in this life.

I like the sweet smell of cows, bitter trampled grass, tangy wet manure, and burning four-wheeler exhaust. I like the sound of bovine hooves falling heavy on the ground and their breathing as their large barrel bodies push forward. When we cut the ignitions on our four-wheelers back up at the barn, you can hear the morning song of a thrush echoing off the dew of the front field. That's something I like too, being able to hear the world—really *hear* it—without the sizzle of electricity moving along power lines or cars crashing down highways or airplanes thundering overhead.

Pop nudges Bert gently into the far milking stall barely avoiding a shit she decides to take as she's settling her head between the stanchions. I release grain for her to eat and then make quick work of wiping each teat with disinfectant before attaching the cups to suck the pearly milk out of her udder. Mandy is up next. On and on we go for the next two hours until finally Frieda makes her way into her milking stall, and I know we're almost done. Pop will take care of letting the rest of the cows back out to pasture, and I'll get to work hosing everything down, cleaning up the spilled milk and shit and grain everywhere.

It has to be seven or so, as I'm pulling off my rubber boots and forcing on my work ones, when Pop says his first words to me. "You comin' up to the house for breakfast?"

"When did you wanna head down to the crick to fix that fence?" I ask.

"Soon as I'm done eatin'."

"Sure then, I'll come up. Won't be able to make it into town for somethin'."

Pop nods and heads for the house, the house I grew up in, the place where he and Mom still live. I can see it through the milk barn office door, a mishmash of red rusty brick, baby blue siding, and a black aluminum roof. The yard needs mowed. There's a swing set out front that seems to be growing out of the weeds. It's for my sister's kids when they visit from the city, not that they've been here for a while. Back off to the side of the house is my mom's garden, the vexation of her existence, even though she plants it every damn year.

I know some people might think it's odd I live only a mile down the road from my folks, and I do spend most of my time on their farm like I've never left the nest. But where else would I go? What else would I do? I like it here. Almost 713 acres all to myself. Best hunting in the county. Quiet. A girl I took out once told me I could do better. She said I ought to go to college and find a "real" job instead of spending all my time fingering cow teats and shoveling their shit. She laughed at me and asked if I had some sort of fetish for cows and shit. I didn't even know what the hell the word fetish meant at the time, but I looked it up after, and well, fuck her.

My family has never had a lot of money, and they never will. Still, we've managed. We eat pretty good, and we set our own schedules. Maybe we don't got a fancy riding lawn mower or a swimming pool or nothing, but there are two cricks that run through our land, three ponds, and a waterfall that will leave a hell of an impression if you're ever lucky enough to see it.

Mom is standing at the stove when I walk in the house. This is how I'll always remember her in the mornings, back turned, eyes focused on something cooking in front of her. This morning it smells like bacon and eggs. I take off my work boots, leave 'em by the door, and take my seat at the kitchen counter. Since I got out of my high chair, I've been sitting in this same exact spot on this same exact stool Pop built for Mom out of old two-by-fours a long time ago.

"You wash your hands?" Mom asks, turning just slightly to see me.

"Yes, ma'am," I say.

"Ambulance was called over to the Mings' place last night. Apparently, Hatcher found Rhett and Shelly laid out in their barn cold to the touch. Overdose is what I heard."

"No way. Not them too."

"Shot 'em full of Narcan and sent 'em up to Springfield."

"Was it heroin?"

"I think it was prescription, but an overdose is an overdose. All I know is Rhett was out for longer than Shelly, and he's been in a coma. They ain't sure he's gonna make it."

"They must've got hooked on that stuff after his car crash," I say, shaking my head at the pity of it all.

"Way it gets passed around here, they coulda got hooked on it at church. Wouldn't be the first time. You still talk to Hatcher?"

"I ain't seen him since he moved out to Rolla," I sigh. "What was he doin' home?"

"Apparently, Rhett and Shelly had been actin' odd, and he drove down to check on 'em."

"Lucky for them he did."

"Well, lucky for Shelly at least," Mom says. "You still goin' giggin' tonight with Miles?"

"Supposed to. Looks like it's gonna be decent weather."

Mom scrapes the fixings out of the cast iron skillet and splits 'em between two plates already set with toast. On cue, Pop walks in and takes *his* place at the counter. Mom slides the plates in front of us, then pours fresh milk into a couple beer mugs she always keeps chilled in the freezer. All that is followed by two steaming cups of Folgers, black as tar and strong enough to just about set the world right.

"Mom tell you about Rhett Mings?" Pop asks. He grabs a bottle of Tabasco to douse his eggs and bacon, then passes it on to me.

"Yeah."

"If people spent half the time workin' they do overdosin', we'd all be a hell of a lot better off around these parts," Pop says, with an exasperated huff.

"People is overdosin' 'cause they ain't got work, Roy. You know that," Mom corrects.

Mom don't eat, don't sit. She pulls on a pair of old, yellow gloves and begins cleaning up the dishes while Pop and me shovel food down our gullets. She'll have her coffee after we're gone, while she sorts coupons and balances the checkbook and goes through the paper to see what's on sale at the supermarket. I think she likes it this way. I know some people would think it's old-fashioned the way we are, but for the most part, none of us would change a thing. Well, no one except my sister, Caitlyn, who thinks she's better than the rest of us—especially Mom—'cause Caitlyn lives in the city where "real things happen." Caitlyn calls herself a feminist, which drives Mom nuts. She don't clip coupons, and her husband, Dan, is the one who cooks for her and her kids. Last time Caitlyn was out here with the boys, she and Mom got into a whole screaming match about how Mom's life ain't gonna add up to nothing 'cause she's only been out of the state twice and to Kansas City one time! Caitlyn has been to New York and Paris, and every year she and Dan take the kids down to Cozumel for summer vacation.

I can't tell if it bothers Mom she's never been much more than a homemaker. I guess that's what you'd call her 'cause out of nothing she's made us—here around this farm—a home. Basically, she had no choice if she was gonna be married to my pop. He told her back when they met, he was saving up to buy a dairy farm—someplace far away from the rest of the world—where he could stretch out, breathe clean air, and watch the sunset unobstructed by so-called civilization. I don't know if she realized then how tough it might get for them, especially when they had kids and their responsibilities extended past their own mouths and hearts to the fruit of their loins. No, I'm sure Mom had no idea what she was in for.

Mom was born Susie Lynn Felton to Thelma and Dewayne Felton of Mountain Grove, Missouri. My grandpa started Felton's Sawmill and ran it all while Mom and her older sister Callie was growing up. Even though them Felton girls was basically reared on sawdust and tree bark, they was thought of as privileged—I guess as much as two girls flouncing around a podunk town could be considered privileged. Still, I can assure you, Mom never let it get to her head that she was better than anyone else, and perhaps it's 'cause she never saw herself as such that she never aspired to some highfalutin life. In fact, after she met my pop in her senior year of high school, all she really aspired to after that was him.

Pop's folks owned a gas pump and general store a few counties over in a place called Blue Moon. Their shack of an establishment was just off the Gasconade River and better known for selling quality fishing bait than just about anything. All while he was growing up, Pop was responsible for making sure the bait tanks was full of minnows, crickets, grasshoppers, and earthworms. Keeping the stink bait stocked was up to my namesake, Pawpaw Honeycutt, who cooked it from a special recipe that made use of turkey livers, deer blood, curdled cheese, flour, and cod liver oil. And it was known by folks all over the state to emit fumes noxious enough, it could knock a grown man right out of his boots.

Pop certainly wasn't any better off growing up than Mom and Aunt Callie, but he weren't much worse off neither. Still, a secondary education wasn't in the cards, and if he wanted to do anything outside of working at the general store—like start himself a dairy farm—he'd have to figure out the means to do so on his own. That's why, not long after finishing high school, he went to work at Felton's Sawmill 'cause he knew he could make himself some good money there—certainly better than what his parents could pay him. And the way he figured it, if he kept his head on and all his fingers in place, in a few years he might have enough saved for a down payment on a grange like he'd been dreaming about practically since he was in diapers.

Of course, working as a log hoist operator for Felton's was when him and Mom started chasing each other around like two squirrels up the same tree. The way I've heard it, their love was about as pure and beautiful as the crystalline icicles that dripped off the rooftop of the sawmill the winter they met. And so, before the first signs of spring, they was married. And maybe if things had gone on the way they was going, those sparkly-eyed newlyweds never woulda had the money to start a proper dairy. But Mom's parents died in a head-on car crash while driving too fast down Route 60, and she took what little they left her and gave it to Pop to secure his dream—a plot of land out in the middle of the boondocks with a milk barn, a couple grain silos, and a proper herd of cattle. In a way, the dairy was her dream by that time too. Yessir, the truth of the matter is Mom chose dairy life when she chose Pop. And just like him, I'm pretty sure she's been happy enough out here in their little corner of the world, her only reprieve being those romance novels she picks up from the library sale bin once a year. And the fact is, I'd say Caitlyn is the one who's really *unhappy* what with all she and Dan's clothes and cars and that house of theirs and even a gardener to mow their grass. Then again, who am I to throw stones? I'm the one who woke up this morning knowing today would be my last.

Somehow Pop always finishes eating before I do, and he says he'll see me up at the barn. Mom immediately begins scouring his plate and milk mug, but he takes his coffee cup with him outside. It's two seconds later when I follow suit.

"Be careful out there on the river tonight," Mom says.

"We will be," I assure her.

"Been forever since your dad and me went giggin'," she sighs. "I miss all that fresh fish on the riverbank."

"Well, we should all go sometime," I say, forgetting for a moment there won't be a next time.

"I doubt your dad would want to. His arthritis. And I haven't been up late enough to gig in twenty years."

For a moment, I look back and watch my mom at the sink. She's a pretty woman, and if you squint just a tad you can almost see her exactly the way she was when she was younger. I see her the way she was back then more than I see her the way she is now. Sometimes, in a certain light, I realize how time has claimed her, but truthfully, I prefer to let my mind erase the wrinkles and sags. Same with my pop and this house and the farm. Only problem is, even if you manage to stop time around this place in your mind, it still rages on outside of here. Sometimes, I feel like we'll be eat up by everything happening just beyond the tree line, all those things I can't erase with my mind no matter how hard I try: Wars. Riots. Floods. Famine. Hate. Anger. Jealousy. Rage. And I'm to blame, they say. Me and Mom and Pop and our farm and our cows and our hunting and our simple way of life. We's what's wrong with the world—especially me, a middle-aged, straight, white man with nothing to my name but a gun and a prayer.

When I get up to the barn, Pop's already got his four-wheeler loaded with barbwire and some tools. "Can't find my damn gloves," he says.

"You can use mine," I offer.

He don't respond. He won't take my gloves. He'd rather string barbwire with his bare hands than accept help from me—from anyone. I move over to my four-wheeler and open the toolbox, make sure I have my come-along, wire cutters, gloves, and hacksaw. "You want me to get a hole-digger?"

"Naw. We won't need it." Pop disappears back into the barn, and I wait. He's looking for his gloves, and I'm kicking myself that I lost my extra pair—he'd take an *extra* pair. I think about going up to the house and asking Mom if she's seen Pop's work gloves, but that would just piss him off and get her a clucking about him being careful with his hands, and how he needs to pay attention to where he puts things.

Our farm dog, Holly, comes walking over to smell my boots and say hi, her tongue lolling out the side of her mouth. She's an Australian Shepherd, shaggy dark grey hair with black spots and no tail. I ain't sure if she was born without a tail or it was cut off when she was young. All I know is we've had her for near eight or nine years now. Got her from the Young's out in Raymondville. They raise the best farm dogs around, real well-behaved and smart. She gets along great with Dixie who'll probably show up here later, make her way through the woods over to Mom and Pop's place. They love it out here, Holly and Dixie. They get to roam free and do their thing, bark at squirrels and deer and keep the coyotes at bay. I think this is the only way to own big dogs like ours. You gotta give 'em space. Never makes sense to me to see these city slickers with retrievers, beagles, and especially shepherding dogs living in tiny apartments, giving 'em two walks a day to shit and pee. Poor things. Seems like torture of a special kind to me, and Lord knows they always have a look of sadness on their faces like they can't quite figure out how they wound up in this special kinda purgatory.

Pop finally emerges from the barn. He found his gloves, throws them in his toolbox with a whispered curse, and we take off for the back hundred. It's an easy ride, and this early in the morning with a full belly and a fall breeze nipping at your face, it's just about perfect. Pop bought the back hundred eight years ago when Kenneth Cantrell died and his kids went to sell it. They didn't know what kinda land they had, all them old oaks worth more than the land itself. But Pop didn't buy it to log it. No, he bought it so from the house every piece of countryside he could see, he owned. He has a certain kinda pride in that. Also, there's a natural spring on Cantrell's that runs through part of the woods before dropping about fifty feet in the most beautiful waterfall you ever seen. Around the base of that waterfall is a natural watering hole for all the wildlife in the area. You go down there any given day, you'll find all kinds of footprints: deer, turkey, coyotes, raccoons, bobcats, bears, and I'm pretty sure we even found a cougar print there one time. I say pretty sure 'cause a few people around the area have said they spotted that ol' cat at one point or another, though me and Pop ain't seen hide nor hair of it and can't independently verify its existence.

According to Pop, the watering hole ain't for hunting. That, he's been very strict about since the day that land officially became ours. And I suppose it ain't fair to put wildlife in fear of one of the only places around they can quench their thirst. Or maybe it's something else I don't understand about that place that has Pop so protective. One time he told me owning that waterfall meant more to him than just about anything else he ever bought 'cause it's not something you find every day. Anybody can own a truck or a house or a piece of land, but who gets a fifty-foot waterfall to call all their own?

Fall has definitely arrived. She's a little late this year, but we had a late spring. Trees don't seem to be turning all the vibrant colors they usually do. They's just dropping their foliage like worn-out garments at the end of a hard day. As such, a grove of cedar trees along the rutted dirt road we're zipping down stand out dark green against the naked oaks and sycamores. You can smell the cedars before you reach 'em, and it's a mighty fine perfume they give off, sweet and oily and seasoned with life. Pop keeps saying he's gonna cut 'em all down 'cause they's crowding out a few dogwoods trying to spring up, but I kinda like 'em and the way their puffy, green jackets absorb all the sound and wind and for a moment—when you're in the middle of 'em—you feel peaceful and protected like an ol' white-tail bedding down for the night.

Just past the cedars is the big hill leading to the bottom. On one side of it is a catfish pond and on the other is one of the cricks we claim as our own. Pop cleared this hill back when he first bought the land. He wanted to return it to native grasses and wildflowers. This was the hill we grew up sledding on, me and my sister and a few of our friends. It was hell to pull the sled all the way up to the top, but it was just about the best kinda fun you can have sledding down. One time during a real good snow we had the Cooper's over and Pop built a bonfire at the base of the hill next to the crick. He used the four-wheeler to haul the sled up the hill for us kids. We cooked hot dogs and marshmallows and made s'mores all under one of the biggest full moons I've ever seen. And one time, when Pop wiped out with the sled at the bottom of the hill, he screamed in awful pain like he'd broken a bone. Mom just about lost it, and everybody came running only to find him red-faced from laughing so hard. He'd do that sometimes, josh around to get a laugh. It was fun to see him smiling like he would during one of his jokes.

At the bottom of the big hill, a crick splits the valley in two. You gotta cross it to get to the other side of the property, and most of the time that ain't a problem unless there's been a big rain. When we was kids my sister and me used to come down here and pick the gooseberries that grow all along the water and try and catch the crawdads without getting bit by their pincers. Back then, there was just a few birch trees that hugged the shoreline, but Pop let 'em grow, and now they's everywhere. Of course, 'cause they's in the bottom, most of 'em still have their leaves, but they'll drop soon. Pop and I cross the crick without a problem 'cause the water is low. Then, we head up and over a rise towards another big pasture Pop plants with a few acres of corn each year to help the wild animals get through the winter.

Holly and Dixie suddenly dart from an area of the woods we call Skunk Ridge. They's running full speed ahead of us, tongues out, smiles on their faces. Pop points to a couple wild turkeys in the far corner of the pasture. They's already ducking their heads and racing for cover when I spot 'em. Holly and Dixie know we're looking at something 'cause they hear our four-wheelers throttle down, but by the time they figure out where we're looking, the turkeys is long gone.

We have to cross another crick before we get to another big hill, the biggest on our property. It'll take us up towards the back hundred. When we went exploring as kids, this was where we always stopped, like the back hundred was cursed in some way, and we shouldn't venture up to it. Perhaps this was 'cause the road also narrows here and the trees seem to reach out with their twiggy fingers kinda ominously. It's also just a damn hard hike to make it up this hill, but the reward for doing so is the best view around. From the top of the back hundred, you can see all the way to the forest tower in Roby, and clear out to the Wright County Line where the Shrodes live.

Pop and me have been trying to clear the top of the back hundred for a few years now, cutting down the trees and bulldozing 'em up into large stacks of logs here and there. Over this last summer, we dug trenches around the brush piles and tried our best to burn 'em down. It's quite the sight to see a half-dozen bonfires big as trailer houses burning on the top of a hillside, especially against the purple sky of nightfall. The sparks all dance up into the air like fireflies, and the blaze casts shadows long as country roads in every direction. Mom invited sis and the grandkids out for the burn this summer. She told Caitlyn we'd get the lawn chairs, make some homemade gooseberry ice cream, and go up and watch the fire. But my sister refused. She said burning the brush was bad for the environment, and bad for the grandkids. She said she didn't understand why Pop would want to go cutting down all those trees for no good reason. This was why we have climate change and tornadoes and hurricanes and stuff 'cause of the destruction of the planet. I gotta admit, I don't honestly know why Pop feels the need to clear the hilltop either. We have enough pastureland for the cows, and Lord knows we ain't growing any crops, but I ain't gonna question Pop's reasoning. It's his land. He's been here longer than any of the rest of us. He can do with it whatever he wants, I suppose. All I know is when we was kids my sister and me used to love watching brush piles burn. We'd get long sticks and poke the tips of them in the embers. Then, when they caught fire, we'd dance with them around the fields watching the tips glow neon orange like magic wands. In our minds, we were characters from another time and world: royalty, adventurers, conductors of any fantasy we could imagine. And it's an honest shame my sister's kids will never have the chance to feel the enchantment we felt on those days. This is why Mom wants me to have kids of my own, so I can raise 'em like she and Pop raised me.

We pass through another hurst of cedars and head down the far side of the back hundred where we finally cross what used to be the property line between Cantrell's land and our own. Here, another crick spans the road. Just before crossing it, we park our four-wheelers and cut the engines. Sublime silence.

"Looked like a couple young gobblers and four hens," Pop says, referring to the turkeys we saw down by the corn rows. He grabs his tools, straining under the weight of a quarter bale of barbwire.

"Looked healthy."

"Yeah, they've been enjoyin' that corn," Pop says.

"Crick's low," I say.

Pop regards the crick, doesn't say anything, which means he disagrees.

As we walk through the woods towards where we's gonna do the fence repair, I wonder if anybody else has ever set foot on the exact spot on earth that I'm now treading. Before Pop had this farm, and before Kenny Cantrell, it belonged to a logging company out of Ohio, but they never logged it for whatever reason. And before that, it must've belonged to the Indians—probably Osage or Cherokee. Whatever the case, these oaks around us have been in this holler for at least three hundred years or so, completely undisturbed, and I feel 'em watching me as though I'm some sorta intruder entering their private world.

Occasionally, I've found ol' arrowheads on our property—signs there was definitely hunting going on around these parts by some form of primitive creature. I know at one time Missouri was full of elk, buffalo, and all sorts of other animals that have either gone extinct or moved on from here. Still, I wish I'd round the corner and find one of 'em—a lynx or a wild horse—who didn't run off, who's still around not knowing that the world outside these woods has changed drastically. And maybe the truth is, me and Pop are the next animals to go extinct from here. And maybe after we're gone people will come through and wonder what *we* were like: farmers, hunters, ignorant white men. Or maybe they'll be glad to see us go extinct 'cause we were never supposed to be here anyway 'cause they think this land don't belong to us. They act like we stole it from the Indians, like we tamed it with slaves—my pop and me. But I had no choice in the matter and neither did he. Still, I guess we pay the price, we take the scorn, even if we don't got no other home. This is where we was born. This is where we was raised. This is where I'll die.

You can hear the waterfall before you see it, and as we get closer, everything turns green again, like fall ain't quite touched this place yet. Ferns sprout up from the forest floor like a grandstand of peacock feathers. Mint-colored lichen grows up the sides of trees and crusts over the north sides of rocks. On the southern end of the waterfall a bunch of lady slipper orchids have taken refuge, their long leopard print leaves feeding off the musty air, fueling 'em up before this whole place turns white and goes dormant for the winter. It's a sight to behold when the waterfall freezes over with icicles twenty feet long dripping down to the pool underneath.

Pop's and my boots mash the expired leaves beneath our feet into the damp earth as we descend around the north side of the falls. Pop is ahead of me and walks over to the black clay bank surrounding the pool looking for animal tracks. In the distance, I hear Holly and Dixie crashing through the woods.

"Damn dogs. They'll scare off everything around," Pop says. Then he grimaces, "Looks like somebody was up here recently."

I see what Pop's found, a small mound of burnt logs and ash, remnants of a fire. There's an empty bottle of Jack Daniel's and a few marijuana butts. Off in a gooseberry bush, I see a used condom hanging from the branches like a translucent worm. Pop sees it as well. He takes the Jack Daniel's bottle, drops each of the marijuana butts inside, then he pulls out his hanky and uses it like a glove to grab the condom, wrap it up, and shove it in his pocket.

"I shoulda got up here last week to fix that fence," he says, and he kicks the mound of burnt logs to disperse them.

"Well, we'll get 'er done now," I assure him.

We follow the water from the pool along the crick to where the fence that cuts across it has been downed. Pop inspects the barbwire like a TV show detective. I know he's wondering if the same folks who built the fire cut through the fence to get up to the waterfall, or if the wire broke 'cause of a tree limb falling on it or the water tugging at it when that last heavy rain came through. Either way, whoever partied up here had to have known what was here and known they was trespassing just the same.

I set down my tools and move over to a tree on one side of the crick where half of the downed barbwire fence is fastened into place. The tree has puckered up around the metal threads, and I remember back to when I helped Pop re-string this fence eight years ago, right after he'd bought the land off Kenny's kids.

Pawpaw Honeycutt had died and Pop got what was left of the ol' general store and homestead over in Blue Moon, which he sold to a hippy couple from California. The husband said he did sound for films out in Hollywood. However, when I asked what movies he'd done sound for, I didn't know any of 'em. Not that I'm some connoisseur of cinema or something. I think the last time I went to a movie was three years ago for a date. We went to the drive-in theater in Raymondville, which shows flicks about six months after they've been released. That means, you might as well stay home 'cause, sure enough, they'll be on TV about the same time you can see 'em at the drive-in. But I guess it ain't the same in a way 'cause the drive-in feels like you're actually doing something as opposed to sitting on your couch. At least that's what the girl I was with said. I think her name was Becky or Brenda or Bethany. Something with a "B." And really, we shoulda just stayed home 'cause no sooner did the picture start than she unzipped my pants and was giving me a blow job, which incidentally wasn't exactly welcome given the fact there was so many people in their cars all around us. Anyway, the hippy couple's check cleared the bank, and Pop used that money to buy the Cantrell's farm. Then, he and Mom pushed some money on me for the down payment on my own place. I'm not sure if they did that so

I would get out of my old room, or so I'd be lonely enough it'd force me to find a wife. Either way, I liked being on my own. Not that much changed. I still got up the same time every morning and went to bed around the same time every night. But now I could walk to the bathroom in my skivvies if I needed to, and I didn't have to worry about the volume on the TV ever being up too loud. And if I had a girl over, well...

You know how they say you never realize life while you're living it? Back eight years ago things was different than they are now. They was good. I mean, we'd all been through the damn recession and survived. Obama even signed a bill giving us dairy farmers 350 million bucks to set our farms upright again. And well, there was hope for us, like everybody in the world suddenly jumping on that Keto Diet and eating cheese like it was going out of style. Fat was good, and city folks wanted milk. Prices were doing fine, and banks were lending us money once more. People was happy. Here, at least locally, everything seemed alright. That was back when my sister, Caitlyn, was pregnant with her first kid, and my high school sweetheart, Mandy, and me had reconnected.

Mandy was the one who reached out. She'd been engaged to marry some idiot outta Springfield. They'd met in college not long after we'd broken things off, just after the end of our senior year. But apparently, despite finishing college and moving in together, they'd split up after he found out she'd made it with another guy, which she told me she only did to get back at him 'cause he was screwing some blonde-haired receptionist at their gym who had "fake tits."

Anyway, I was happy to hear from her. And by the time we started "hanging out" again, she'd moved out to Rolla where she was teaching third grade. On Saturday's when Pop had Kyle Hanky come over to fill in for me at the milk barn, I'd drive out to see her, and boy-o-boy, we had some good times. She was always raring to get into bed first thing. And damn, she knew what she was doing. Blew my mind how adventurous she was, and how much she'd learned. Certainly more than any other girl I'd dated, and more than I ever thought I would know. Then after she'd tire herself out, we'd grab Sonic or Kentucky Fried Chicken and head over to Little Prairie Lake to sit and watch the sunset. Of course, that's when the tears would start, her getting all emotional about the past, talking about how she'd messed up with me and then with that dumbass, Frank. Somehow, I knew from the way she went on that I was just a band-aid until she picked up the pieces and found herself again as well as somebody new. I would never be enough for her now.

Going to college she'd decided on some big ideas that were bigger than me, a simple dairy farmer. I was like a glass of warm milk in the middle of the night, something to soothe her temporarily. But we'd had our time already. In high school, we fit perfectly together, everything so novel to both of us, all our hopes and dreams so far from reality, they didn't really matter. What mattered was the comfort of each other in the middle of pop quizzes and tests and report cards and school dances. We weren't going anywhere back then, not really. And all the things we shared in common were by default: the teachers we didn't like, the gossip we did, the drama, the laughs, the easy delight of a summer afternoon. Then, the end seemed to come barreling up on us like a combine eating up the last patch of corn, severing it from its life source, tumbling it, shredding it, whittling it down to practically nothing. Mandy was accepted to college up in Springfield, and I was just gonna stay working at the dairy like I always had. Sure, there were a few discussions about trying to keep things going long distance. But we knew the truth. The call had been made for us, and like a crick splitting off in the woods, we was aware our life journeys' was carrying us in two very different directions.

That's what I understood the second time we started things up too, and what I tried to help Mandy realize. But she didn't want to hear it. So, we'd fight over our nonexistent future and over our differences of opinion about stuff, which by that time was everything. She listened to music I'd never heard of, and I still liked jokes she no longer appreciated. Looking back now, maybe I coulda tried harder to see her side of things, but she didn't really want to put in the work of waiting for me to catch up to her. Honestly, I don't know if I ever would have. When I told her my folks had given me the down payment for the little house a stone's throw from their farm, that's when I think she realized things for me was just like they'd always been; I was a farmer plain and simple.

The last time we saw each other, she came to visit my new place, and help me "fix it up." Right away I could see from the squint in her eyes and the way she bit her bottom lip that she didn't approve. Still, she tried to be positive. She was determined to convince me to rip out the ol' carpet in the living room, tile the bathroom, paint everything inside and out, and buy a bunch of new appliances for the kitchen. I talked her into a little cleaning and a new microwave. That night, after we'd put away the Windex and Comet and vacuum, I'd borrowed from my mom, I built us a bonfire out in the backyard, and I held Mandy in my lap. We didn't talk. We just stared at that bonfire. There wasn't any sex when we went to bed neither. And when I came back from milking cows the next morning, she was gone. For some reason, I knew not to text her, and she didn't text me. And that was that.

I shoulda known all the hope I had then was pointless. I mean, buying a house around this area is like running a farm. It's a losing proposition. Of course, you don't realize that until way too late. By 2012, all them Keto nuts started drinking almond milk. Then came oat milk, cashew milk, and coconut milk, and just about every other kind of milk you can imagine, including hemp. Then, the USDA goes and bans whole milk in schools altogether. Hell, it wasn't even just whole milk, it was 2% and 1%. Not to mention the EPA suddenly running around telling us farmers we're ruining the rivers 'cause our manure lagoons aren't up to snuff. And we small-time guys don't have the means to fight back like the big operations who are the ones really doing all the damage. And fuck it all, if I hadn't voted for that Obama twice! Suddenly, I understood why people railed against him like they did. It wasn't just 'cause he was letting the gays marry, but 'cause of what he did to us in the rural areas, especially us dairy farmers. Then, there was that whole brouhaha about confiscating guns. I don't know if it was true or not. Didn't matter really. He and his administration took the only thing that meant something to us when they cut off our dairies at the knees. They took our well-being. Nothing's ever free, I guess, especially 350 million bucks.

I hear Pop let out a sharp sigh, and I look over to see him shaking off a sting from one of the barbs. He's trying to get all the old wire lassoed up before we start stringing the new stuff.

"You want to make it three lines like before?" I ask.

"Might as well," he says.

I start binding a new piece of barbwire to the top strand of the old stuff. Then, I tack it to the tree for good measure.

"I'll tell you what, I wind up brain dead for whatever reason, I don't want to spend a single day with tubes shoved up every hole I got and machines keeping me on life support," Pop says.

I know he's thinking about Rhett and Shelly Mings. He's probably been stewing on that all morning. "Awe, you'll outlive everybody, Pop," I assure him.

"I sure hope not. The older you get the faster life happens but the slower you move through it. Some days it's just too damn painful."

"I hear you," I say, and I toss the wire I was working with across the crick to Pop so he can tighten it up on the other side.

"Besides, makin' a livin' has gotten too damn hard for farmers nowadays," Pop says. "I can't even imagine doin' it with any fewer facilities than the ones I barely got as it is. That's why I'm ready to be rid of this whole damn operation. Lord knows with the way them liberals talk about milk, soon they'll be tellin' everybody milk ain't just cow pus, it's actual poison. And then what are we gonna do? I'm tired of goin' into debt more and more each year while all them elected jokers use our government subsidies like poker chips in their stupid political games. It's got to the point, I can't sleep no more."

I think about the antacids I took a few hours before. And suddenly, I'm wishing I had 'em with me.

"And hell, I get it," Pop continues. "I mean, a handout to us ain't no different than a handout to some folks poorer than we are."

"It *is* different, though, Pop," I say. "Them folks, they don't work as hard as we do. What we do is essential to life continuin' for people on this planet."

"Maybe," he says, and he starts tightening the wire with the come-along.

I watch him for a moment, astonished at his strength for an arthritic fifty-eight-year-old man. And I think of Mandy again and how she would have chewed me out for saying people on welfare don't work hard or don't want to work. Caitlyn woulda been all over me too. They woulda asked me what the hell I wanted to see happen to people who got nothing, just let 'em starve?

"Besides, you can't sell the farm. You do that, I won't have a job," I say.

"Awe, you could make more money if you went and worked over at the farm supply in Licking. Or Danny Reeds would probably hire you over at his outfit. He's the only one crazy enough to expand, right now, *and* the means to do it."

"Pop, we could expand. Maybe sell Cantrell's here, buy more cows, update the equipment."

"I'm not sellin' Cantrell's. *That*, I am not doin'!" Pop says emphatically. "This place with these trees and that waterfall, it's been my favorite spot in the world since I first laid eyes on it forty years ago."

"Use it as collateral then."

"I wish I could," Pop says. "Wouldn't change much. I just can't compete with all these damn CAFO's and the Danny Reeds of the world. You ain't gonna be able to neither, even if we got three hundred more head of cows."

I want to throw my hammer at him. I want to clobber him, stubborn ol' awful coward. He talks a big game, but the truth is, he wouldn't sell the dairy any sooner than I would. Then suddenly, I double over in pain 'cause still, I know what he's saying is true. "Fuck!" I scream.

Pop looks over at me knowing what's going on, "You got those pains again?"

Tears fill my eyes, but I won't let them fall. I nod, keeping the agony of my face away from him.

"This is what I'm tellin' you, Calem. None of this, it ain't worth it."

"Fuck you, Pop. This is all *you* know, and this is all *I* know, and this is all *I want to know*!"

"Hand me that wire," he says, and he holds out his hand for me to toss him the next rung of barbwire I just finished nailing to the tree.

"Look, I just think it's good for us to consider options. I ain't goin' down to the courthouse to declare bankruptcy like so many others is. We ain't those type of people to go renegin' on our word. If I got nothin', I still got my name."

It takes us another forty minutes to finish the patch of fence over the crick, and neither of us says another word the whole time. Meanwhile, I honestly ain't sure if I'm gonna wretch my breakfast or shit it out the other end. When we finally pack up our things and pass back by the waterfall, Pop stops to take a drink, and I do the same. And I think, that's the thing; it's hard work doing what we do, being who we are, but damn, who else is serenaded by the sounds of nature all day long and cooled by the breeze of an air so fresh you think it's gotta be from the flapping of angel's wings? Who gets to drink out of their own private waterfall anytime they want? Then suddenly, a wave of frigid water comes at me, soaking me all down my front. I look over at Pop who's laughing his ass off, stepping away from the water so I can't splash him back. I know what he's trying to tell me; cool down, everything's gonna be okay. And at that moment, I love him. I love that ol' stubborn, arthritic man.

When Pop and me get back to the house, Mom is outside with Delmar Munson and his shiny, red semi-trailer truck. He's sporting a fresh buzzcut, Oakley sunglasses, and starched Levi's, strutting his stuff like a barnyard cock. Apparently, he's already pumped last night and this morning's milk from the barn to the massive stainless steel tank he hauls around all day. I know it irritates Pop that Delmar is early and Mom is out chatting him up. But somehow, he's always early on Fridays and Saturdays, probably 'cause he wants to get everything finished and get to the good part of the weekend, which for him is not working. Mom and Delmar turn to us as we pull up, and I can immediately tell from the strained smile on Mom's face something ain't right. I know Pop sees it too.

Pop parks and walks over to Mom and Delmar. "You're always early on the weekends, Delmar."

Mom crosses her arms and sighs, "Plant is sayin' they're gonna stop sendin' Delmar all the way out here to pick up our milk."

All the ease Pop is tryin' to play instantly disappears. "That's horsepucky."

"Trust me, I'm as confused as anyone," Delmar says, and he kicks the ground with his boot.

"Why would they send you to tell us somethin' like that?" Pop asks.

"They didn't. I'm just relayin' what I overheard," Delmar shrugs, clearly feeling awful about it. "Nobody knows I know."

"We're one of the oldest stakeholders of that cooperative," Pop spits.

"Trust me, I get it." Delmar holds his hands up in surrender. "But, you're also the only farm out in these parts nowadays. And apparently, people think it just ain't worth it to send a truck out here no more, especially when it's just for barely a quarter tank of milk."

Slowly Pop's face falls as though finally comprehending what Delmar is trying to relay to him. Up until this moment, I'm not sure even I fully grasped that we were really *the last* dairy farm out here in Texas County.

"Now, there's that cooperative down near Paul's Bluff. I'm pretty sure they'd be open to workin' with you. They's all about smaller farms, and they pay their members well," Delmar offers.

"They're all organic. I can't afford to switch everythin' over to organic. That'd take three years. Two at least," Pop says, shaking his head.

"I'm just sayin' there's options."

"Where did you hear they're votin' us out?" Pop asks again.

Delmar shakes his head, looks Pop in the eyes. "I can't say. And you can't tell 'em I told you so neither. But I go way back with y'all, and if what I heard is the truth, I wanted y'all to be prepared."

"I'll call Bill over there and clear this whole thing up this afternoon. You sure what you heard?" Pop asks.

Delmar nods. "Look, I'm takin' your milk, right now. You still own a piece of that co-op just like everybody else, but when things come up for a vote next meetin', you need to be ready."

Pop looks at Mom who can offer him no consolation. Then, he looks at me with his blue eyes wide and crazed.

"We'll figure this out, Pop," I promise, but I don't think he hears me.

Delmar walks around to the cab of his truck and hops behind the wheel. Then, he closes the door and leans out the window. "Now you remember, you didn't hear any of this from me." The truck lets out a hiss as Delmar releases the brakes and takes off down the road.

I turn from watching Delmar's shiny red truck disappear back to Pop, but he's already halfway across the yard, stomping away.

"Mom, we'll figure it out," I say.

"You hungry? You need some coffee?" she asks, brushing a wisp of hair out of her face.

I shake my head. "Tell Pop I borrowed a tarp if you see him. Be back in a couple hours. I'm takin' that trailer full of walnuts over to Kell's."

I head for the barn, and I know Mom is watching me as I walk away. I know she wishes I'd say something that'd make her feel better, just like I wish she had some words for me, just like Pop wishes somebody had comfort for him. But there is none. Not for folks like us. Not anymore. Our very lives have become just like every other damn thing on a farm: a fence that needs fixed, a tree that needs cutting down, a truck that needs worked on, a cow that needs help delivering her calf. But I'd prefer to have my arm halfway up a cow's ass, pulling out a calf that's strangling on its own umbilical cord, anything other than being told you got no hope. And here I was thinking I had no hope this morning, but boy-o-boy, that pales in comparison to how I'm feeling now.

As I enter the barn, I grab a wheel barrel, lift it up and heave it across the room, causing it to spark when it hits the cement floor with a crash. This act of anger feels good for only one second, then it's followed by that damn pain. I double over, holding my gut, trying not to scream out.

Holly and Dixie poke their heads around the barn door to check on me. They know something is up, and they gently wander over to lick my trembling hands. To be honest, I don't want their love. I don't want anything other than to not feel like shit and smell like shit and look at shit. I sit down against one of the milking stalls and put my cap over my face to block everything out. But Holly and Dixie are too concerned for me to leave me alone. Their wet muzzles press all over me. Their dog-breath tongues that smell like warm milk lick me up and down.

God, where are you? I ask in my head. *What about the little sparrow, God? Ain't we at least as important as the sparrow?*

The truth is, I don't really believe in God or heaven or hell or any of that mumbo jumbo. I go to the same Presbyterian church in town Mom and Pop go to, but I don't give religion a whole lotta mind. Maybe I should. And maybe if I did, I would be more concerned about what comes after a person goes boots up. But farmers ain't got time for concerns like that. To a farmer, the future ain't no further out than the next rainfall or lightning storm or sunrise. People think all us folks here in the Midwest is holier-than-thou wingnuts, but that just ain't true. I'd say first and foremost, we is just traditionalists who think if it ain't broke, don't fix it. I guess though, what I'm realizing lately is, it *is* broke, the whole fucking lot of it. And something's gotta change for everybody. But for whatever reason, it feels like the answer ain't out there, at least not for *me*. It ain't Black Lives Matter and the transgenders and gun control and regulations up the wazoo. How is any of that gonna fix *my* situation? Everyone is telling me I gotta look out for everybody that ain't a white, straight, gun-toting, undereducated man, but who's looking out for *me*? They fucked me over too, whoever they is that's fucking over everyone else, I'm telling ya. We're all in this damn boat together. And that boat is sinking under the weight of the tears of its passengers, capsizing into an ocean filled with the bodies of all those who've come before us.

I always believed the dead were supposed to prop us up, guide our souls towards light and goodness, but I'm starting to realize all they do is pull us down and steer us off course. And we let them. We listen to their every whisper from the grave, memorizing it, branding it on our hides. All of us humans alive on this planet is faltering because of them—every color, sex, and creed that's come from every color, sex, and creed. Their pain begets our pain. Their loss begets our loss. Their anger begets our anger. Their grief begets more and more and more grief until maybe one day the remaining fragments of our so-called humanity will finally dissolve into the gutless cauldron of wickedness our forbearers cooked up for us. And then—maybe then—the earth can start over clean and new with purity and magic and angels—*Hallelujah!*—without all the hurt that reflects hurt out into an infinitude of space and time that will never find a salve as long as we are here, as long as we remain human. We are all the wrongly spent deed of life. We are the subtraction of our own glory. From Adam and Eve on, we've been made so. We've accepted the mold our makers poured for us. Before we even knew we existed, they demanded we be their mirror. And so blinded by their images we stare out in every direction from the black hole of our suffering, speaking in tongues that tear us apart, using words that leave gaping wounds in our souls, decimating each other with our actions. How do I know these things, stupid hick that I am? We all know them, don't we? All these gospels planted inside us, the anima and animus of our ancestors. Close your eyes, and it's there—a kaleidoscope of truth and lies. But which do you choose? How do you parse the fact from fiction? Right from wrong? How do you move forward? When your eyes open again, how do you alter course on a planet spinning ever more out of control?

When I stand back up a few minutes later and readjust my cap, Holly and Dixie seem satisfied they've done their job and made everything better. So, off they trot. I'm still in a daze, though, as I head over to one of the storage rooms where I know Pop keeps a couple tarps to cover hay bales in the winter and whatnot.

The tarps is exactly where I suspect they will be, and I grab the smallest one—a bright blue one that smells like old motor oil and cat piss. I throw it in the bed of my truck and toss my tackle box on top of it so it won't blow out. It's eleven o'clock now; I can easily make it over to Kell's with the walnuts, then back in time for milking at five—maybe grab a bite at Patty's. I look around the yard to see if Pop is anywhere, but there ain't hide nor hair of him.

Driving along the dirt road out towards the highway, I leave the windows on the truck down and let the fall air blow against my face. It's sweet and clean and calms my nerves. I think about how Pop suggested we sell the cows and the equipment, and I wonder if maybe I shouldn't have argued with him about that. I only did so 'cause I was thinking about his well-being even more than my own. He wouldn't know what to do without the dairy, no matter what he says. Maybe I should tell him I think it's a bright idea to cash out. He and Mom could retire and enjoy their lives a little. Hell, if they sell everything, they might even be able to put some money in their pockets and keep Cantrell's. As for me, he don't need to be worried. I ain't gon' be around much longer anyways. I've made up my mind on that. If anything, Delmar's warning only confirms what I've been feeling, that I got no place in this world no more.

There's a turnout where my folks' dirt road hits the paved highway up ahead. The turnout leads to an old, white clapboard church that sits in the middle of a small field at the front of my parents' property. The chapel looks like it's straight off one of them calendars they give you at the bank, and today, in particular, it stands out like the white tail of a doe. It's a one-room structure with a steeple over the front doors, tall as the building itself, and an old black bell still hanging in the belfry just slightly cocked to one side. The church was part of the land back when Mom and Pop bought the farm, though it ain't been used by anybody since long before they moved in. There is all kinds of stories about how it was part of the underground railroad during the Civil War, a distillery during Prohibition, a hideout for Jesse James, and finally a rural schoolhouse before it was decommissioned sometime in the seventies. I honestly don't know if any of the stories are true. All I know is, it was built real well 'cause all these years later, it's still moored to the ground, strong as the convictions of those folks who built it. And Mom makes sure it's kept up, all the wavy glass in the windows clean and the lacquered wood floors shined up for when people around the area want to rent it out for "country weddings" and senior photo shoots and all.

Back when we was kids, Caitlyn and I used the church like a playhouse, pretending we was Daniel Boone hiding out from the Indians. We'd haul the farm cats up there with us and dress 'em in Caitlyn's baby doll clothes like they was our kids. Then, we'd boil water on the ol' kerosine furnace inside and fill that water with scraps from Mom's garden, pretending like we was making soup. When we got older, our playing fell off. At a certain point, Caitlyn didn't want nothing to do with her idiot kid brother anymore or pretending to be anything other than the woman she was determined to be. She started hiding away in her bedroom to read every book she could get her eyes on, and the rest of the time she was trying on Mom's makeup and face creams when Mom wasn't around. For a while, I still went up to the church by myself. That's where I first started thinking about girls, spending such inordinate amounts of time by myself in that sanctuary one would have rightly suspected I was giving myself over to the priesthood or would soon turn myself blind. Luckily, the older I got the more Pop needed me around the farm. And when I couldn't be of use to him, I started mowing lawns for the elderly ladies in town and cutting and selling cords of firewood the rest of the time.

Still, neither me nor Caitlyn ever forgot the church. That's where Caitlyn got proposed to by her husband Dan one summer when they was both here on a break from college. And two years later, that's where they got married. As for me, that's where Mandy and me would go strip each other down and make love while we was in high school. I haven't been inside that church in years, but as I watch it recede in the rearview mirror, I suddenly wish I woulda stopped in there just now. I'd love to see if I could find where I carved me and Mandy's initials on the back of the alter and if that bottle of whiskey I stole from the grocery store back when me and Miles was sixteen is still hidden inside the clanky upright piano.

The trailer I've loaded full of walnuts is sitting off to the side of my house, just like I left it yesterday afternoon. The mounds of drupes with their soft green hulls look like tennis balls waiting to be served. The ones on bottom have been there since I started picking about a week or so ago, and their outer flesh is already turning to inky mush. I back right up to the coupler hitch. Then, I check to see if I made it close enough to the trailer, so I won't have to pull forward and back up again. Luckily, I did. I made it *real* close. So, I unwind the jack on the trailer, letting the coupler slide right over the ball.

Seconds later, I'm inside the house, grab more jerky, and pour myself the rest of the coffee in the pot. It's cold, but I'll drink it anyway. For a moment, I stand and look at the house, and I'm proud of what I've done with the place, regardless of what Mandy thought all those years ago. It's peaceful and calming, filled with old furniture from yard sales and flea markets that could tell a million different stories. This last few weeks, I've been cleaning things real good, preparing everything so Mom won't have much of a mess when I'm gone, so they can sell everything as quick as possible. Hell, maybe whoever buys the house will take all the furniture with it. That'd sure make things simple. Suddenly, I realize how eerily quiet this house is too, and I throw back the last of my coffee and head outside.

The sun is already tilting towards sunset, even though it ain't yet noon. The sky is robin's egg blue, and there ain't a cloud in sight. I grab the tarp out of the truck bed, throw it over the walnuts, and tie it down. I doubt any of my little treasures will fall off, but you never know if I'll have to swerve or something 'cause of a pothole or a critter in the road. A walnut flying at a car behind me would probably leave a pretty nice ding, and you know there will absolutely be some yahoo tailing me all the way to Kell's, refusing to pass, but still trying to make a point that I ain't going fast enough. Well, you know what, asshole, I'm going as fast as a person should hauling a forty-eight-foot-long trailer!

Back when Caitlyn and me was kids, we'd pick up walnuts all around my parents' farm to make a little money we could spend on Christmas presents and whatnot. It took the two of us twice as long to fill a trailer half-full than it does for me to fill a whole trailer to overflowing now. Part of the reason had to do with the fact there ain't as many trees on Mom and Pop's land as my little homestead here, but also, we was just so tiny. Still, we worked our hearts out. We didn't wear gloves and our entire arms and faces would be covered in the black stain from the hull juice. One time, Mom wouldn't even wash my clothes 'cause they were soaked through and had turned inky brown and smelled painfully bitter. "We'll just have to throw 'em away," she said. And that's what she did.

For all intents and purposes, Mom is a practical woman. Even when she does something like throw all your clothes away, there's usually a good reason for it. In the case of the walnuts, she was afraid the stains in my clothes would ruin her washing machine and countless other garments before all was said and done. She was always thinking two steps ahead of everyone else. I suppose that's the secret to being successful at just about anything, always thinking two steps ahead. And that's the way Mom was while we were growing up—still is. Hardly never was there a time when Caitlyn or myself or Pop needed something that she didn't have it handy. There was baking soda for yellow jacket stings and bacon fat for cooking up fresh fish. Just about the same day I'd find a hole in one of my socks there was a whole new package of 'em washed and tucked into my underwear drawer. And I swear every time I had my heart broken by some girl, I'd come home to fresh pie and homemade ice cream as though she could foresee what was gonna happen. And the coffee—well, there was always Folgers in the pot next to the phone in the kitchen, fresh and hot.

Don't get me wrong, Mom was far from perfect. She was hella moody sometimes just like the heifers could get. And it didn't always appear there was any reason for it. Maybe it was her moon time. I don't know. But she'd get super quiet like a mouse and barely talk or look at anyone. And I learned early on to tiptoe around her during these periods 'cause if you got on her nerves, boy-oh-boy, she'd suddenly come after you hollering and screaming and listing every damn thing you ever done to piss her off as though she'd been bottling up her rage for years. During those bouts of anger, we called her our "silly goose" what with the way she honked and blustered and seemed ready to hit a person over the head with one of her kitchen cleavers if they came too close. Then later, she'd apologize real simple and quick for losing her temper and go back to her normal self, acting like nothing was wrong, like she hadn't been batshit crazy.

For all the work Pop did on the farm, none of it woulda mattered much if Mom hadn't known how to take what little he pulled in and stretch it, making it work for our family of four. She clipped every coupon she ever came across. Any coupons she couldn't use, she'd trade with other ladies in town during one of their afternoon coffees. Early on, she made Pop buy her a deep freeze so she could get items on sale, freeze 'em, and thaw 'em out later when we might need 'em or want 'em. She canned just about everything in the garden we couldn't eat fresh, so even come the hollow of winter, we always had corn, green beans, carrots, and fruit preserves. Damn, those fruit preserves were about the absolute best thing you could imagine to slather on a warm biscuit or piece of homemade bread. There was an apple tree in one of the pastures we used to pick apples from all the time before it got struck by lightning. Mom used to make everything with them apples: pies, cobblers, apple sauce, apple butter, fried apples, and even cinnamon apple ice cream. I don't know what it cost her to feed us, but she did a lot with whatever Pop gave her, which couldn't have been much. Trust me, I know. I can barely scrape by with what he gives *me*. But that ain't 'cause he's stingy. That's just how things are around here.

Mom's favorite time of year is Christmas, but it's also when I see her struggle the most, see her try to be happy when I know, in truth, she's reminded just how little she and Pop get by on. Growing up, they couldn't afford the laptop computer Caitlyn asked for or the new scope I wanted for my Smith & Wesson. I'm not sure there's ever been a Christmas Pop has bought Mom something nice, not even perfume or a piece of jewelry. Of course, she always smiled watching us kids open new winter coats and dress shoes—"practical presents"—but I knew an hour or so later, she would be quietly crying in the shadows of her and Pop's bedroom 'cause Pop didn't give her a thing...yet again. I don't think this was 'cause Pop wanted to hurt Mom. I just don't think he had it in him to drive to a store and pick something out for her. Maybe it was too overwhelming. Or maybe he felt like the best gift he could give her—could give any of us—was to keep the farm going, to keep the bills paid, to keep food on the table, to give us hope for the future.

I feel like all of us have let Mom down, over and over again through the years, but even still, she's never seemed to waver in her devotion to us or the farm. Even all this time later, having never had a real vacation, having never visited some exotic country like Caitlyn and Dan and their kids. Having never put her feet in an ocean, Mom remains the backbone of the whole operation, probably knowing that she has to keep the ship steady or else the whole thing would fall to pieces in all the storms we've weathered. Two steps ahead, that woman. That's what I'm telling you.

Driving out to Kell's, I know I'll pass three different dairy farms that have shut down over the last few years, their grain silos standing like gravestone markers of their passing. While most of the folks that used to run 'em have been absorbed out into the world somewhere, the farms remain to haunt the rest of us here with all the possibility of what will never be. It's amazing how one day a person can be your friend and neighbor, someone you can count on to borrow jumping cables, who'll come feed your cows when your leg gets broken, or tow you out of a ditch when the roads freeze over, then the next day they're out there in the "real world," another cog in the wheel of meaninglessness. At least that's what it seems to be to me, all that out there—meaninglessness.

The Cooleys' farm is the first one I pass. It's real pretty, up on a hill, overlooking the cow pastures. It had been in the family for decades until Ron and Wendy had three daughters and none of 'em wanted to stick around to work it. They was all handsome girls who were cordial as milk barn cats. They were the type of girls men remembered their manners for. I myself had a slight dalliance with the youngest one, Angela. She was home from college and trying to figure out the next steps for her life when we ran into each other at the filling station. Against her parents' wishes, she'd studied creative writing, she said. According to her, there were no jobs for creative writers unless you managed to write a book, which she was attempting to do, and which she read to me one time after we'd hooked up. I wanted to like it. I really did. But it didn't make a lot of sense, some story about sex trafficking and a brotherhood of truck drivers who were vigilantes. When I told her I thought it was good, apparently, she could see through my lie. Well, clearly offended, she told me I didn't know good writing and that the whole story made perfect sense; she'd researched it and everything! That was the first and last time we took a roll in the hay together.

All these years later, I ain't heard nothing in the gossip chain about Angela finally getting her book published. So, who knows? Maybe nobody else cared much for her book either. I *do* know after signing all the loans so their girls could go off to college, Ron and Wendy couldn't keep up the two hundred heifers they owned. Then, with all the regulations, clean water acts and such, that kept being forced on 'em from the government, they couldn't afford to upgrade their equipment. Instead of going bankrupt, one day they just up and sold off everything piecemeal and moved away without telling anyone where they was going. The folks, Gary and Donna Cordelly, who bought the farm, got it for half of what it was worth. He was gonna goat farm. But of course, that enterprise folded within a year, and they was evicted by the bank. Now the place sits empty like an inverted sinkhole ready to swallow whoever else might come along.

About ten more minutes down the highway is the second place that closed up shop—well, kinda. It belongs to a couple women from Chicago who quit their jobs as lawyers and thought they'd make a go of it down here in the Ozarks running a dairy. They never said they was lesbians, but I'm pretty sure they are. When they bought their farm about thirteen years ago, they flipped it from a beef cattle outfit to a dairy and built the whole thing from the ground up with a new barn and new equipment and all new heifers. And for a while, it seemed like maybe they was on to something 'cause they didn't seem to have any problems at all. Then, things broke down, cows had to be replaced, dairy prices dropped, regulations went up, and the next thing everybody knew those gals quit the dairy business and started practicing law again, setting up shop in their new, old barn. And lucky for them, apparently people around here need lawyers just as much as they do in the big city 'cause those two seem to be hanging onto their farm, even if they lost the dairy itself.

And that's just one of the things that gets me worked up, how people think we don't like homosexuals out here in the country. At least that's what my sister Caitlyn says. In all honesty, I'm pretty damn near fine with 'em—the gays. I don't get it, being attracted to someone who's the same sex as you, but I feel like they all seem happy and smart and like good people, so who really cares who they love? Perhaps it would creep me out if I knew a guy was looking me over like a piece of chicken fried steak, but I've never really known when a girl was checking me out. So, who knows? Maybe I'm just dumb, but my mind don't operate on the assumption that everyone is wanting to have sex with everybody else all the time. I suppose that's why most girls have always had to put the moves on me first, and why those moves have always surprised me. Like when Mandy and I started being together, it was her who came up to me one day before Mr. Slater's chemistry class and asked if I wanted to go down to the river that weekend with her and a couple other kids. And then, when we got down to the river, it was her who pulled me aside in the woods, kissed me, and grabbed my dick through my Wranglers. In all honesty, I'd probably just laugh if a guy ever came on to me 'cause it seems so hilarious to me, two guys wanting to be sexual together. But I've chuckled a bit at how serious girls take sex sometimes too, how they's so territorial and want you to do specific things to them, and always—*always*—they's wanting you to be more aggressive. *"Be more aggressive!" "Be more aggressive!" "Tell me dirty things!" "Choke my neck!" "Slap my ass!"* I have had more than one girl get angry at me 'cause I'd giggle at what she wanted me to do to her or what she wanted to do to me. Then, they'll grab their clothes and storm off and act all hurt. I swear, for being one of the most simple acts one mammal can perform with another, sex is literally the most complicated thing in the world when it comes to human beings.

And now there's all these other considerations to take into account, like if something you say is "sexist" 'cause it makes some girl feel less than a guy. Well, I'll tell you what, I've been made to feel less than by plenty of girls, and that ain't sexism, it's just them being mean. But nowadays, they can get away with it 'cause us guys have had all the power for far too long, they say. "Down with the patriarchy!" That's what one of my sister's T-shirts reads. Well, "patriarchy" was another word I had to look up. And hey, I get it, men have been the bosses forever, but just like so many other things guys like me get accused of, I didn't make it that way. And maybe men before me used to benefit from it, but not me. Hell, I ain't ever looked down on a girl 'cause she was a girl. If anything, I've give 'em more respect. But apparently, even that is sexist now, just like opening the door and paying for dinner. It's all so confusing. And honestly, that's another reason I don't want to be in this world any longer. I'd like to settle down and get married, but I just don't know how to make that happen. Seems like every move I take towards that ideal these days, I'm stepping on somebody's toes or getting accused of something I ain't ever even done.

The last girl I went out with texted me that she was going to tell the sheriff I'd raped her after I said she couldn't spend the night at my house. Thing is, I needed a little sleep before I had to get up and milk the cows the next morning, and that's why I took her home. Still, it was positively insane and scared the shit outta me, I'll tell you what. We'd met at Walmart where she works in the pharmacy. I was picking up Pop's arthritis medication, and there was no one else in line. So, she kept talking and talking, and then she said I should take her number and ask her to dinner, which I did. Well, I shoulda known she was a little fishy when I was late to pick her up and she started pouting about how I wasn't making her a priority. I told her that wasn't true. I'd blown a tire on the truck just as I was leaving Mom and Pop's after milking, and I had to put on a spare. I said I guess if I hadn't cared to shower, I woulda been on time, but then I woulda smelled to high heaven, which probably wouldn't have made her very happy either. She complained about dinner. Then she complained about there being nowhere to dance in town. So, we went back to my place, and I put on some music, which she complained about too. Then, she told me she wanted me to fuck her. Well, I agreed to that, looking forward to showing her something I knew she couldn't complain about. I thought she was real happy when it was all over too. Then, I told her I had to take her back to her place 'cause I needed to get some sleep. And it *was* four hours after my usual bedtime, but truth be told, I couldn't put up with much more of her that night neither. When I dropped her off, she wanted me to promise we'd go out to the lake the next weekend and do some fishing together, which I guess I should've said yes to 'cause when I wouldn't make that promise, well, that sent her off in a huff. And no sooner was I back home in bed than I got her text message telling me she was going to the sheriff's office. Needless to say, I didn't get no sleep that night, and that's when my stomach pains started in real serious like—almost a year ago.

A few miles before I reach the turnoff for Kell's Walnuts, I see the Davis' farm, which shut down just three months ago. It's probably the saddest story of all the places around here 'cause the fact of the matter is Chuck's wife, Leanne, got thyroid cancer. And they was both determined she would beat it. Nowadays there's all sorts of treatments for all the different cancers, and it don't have to be the death sentence it once was, they said. They started a GoFundMe page and there were a couple pancake breakfasts in town to raise money. But it wasn't near enough for the speciality treatments that would save her, the ones that weren't covered by Obamacare. Still, they tried to do what they could. In the end, they sold every last thing they owned and moved in with her folks down in Arkansas in order for her to try an experimental drug that only prolonged her life by a few weeks, according to what I heard. As for Chuck, he plum dropped off the map after that, and the new folks who bought the Davis' farm is a dentist and his wife who have no interest in dairying, but own a couple real beautiful Appaloosas they take riding on the trails around here.

One would think with all the dairies closing up shop our farm would be raking in the dough, but, unfortunately, that ain't how it works. Every time a small dairy folds, it just makes room for one of the big milking operations to stretch out and take up more space, which is exactly what they do. And unlike small dairies, the big guys have enough product they can dictate pricing and monitor supply. It's kinda like everything in life nowadays, the rich keep getting richer and the powerful get more power. And there ain't nothing any of the rest of us can do about it, not really. First of all, unlike the rest of the businesses in America, agriculture don't have a cap on how much a single company can own of our food supply. As such, unless you're part of a powerful co-op, you ain't got a prayer. 'Cause the top four companies in America run the board. They own over eighty-two percent of all the steers and heifers, and half of *those* companies *also* have their fingers and toes dipped in corn and soy, which feed those cows, as well as the supermarkets that sell most of the steak and burger we consume. That means the rest of us is wrestling for scraps from a massive table ain't none of us ever gonna see the top of. And that's why even co-ops, large as the one Pop has been a part of since he started his dairy thirty years ago, have a hard time competing 'cause they're still so small in comparison to the big guys. That's why even *our* co-op is saying they have to trim the fat, or in our case—and the cases of so many others around this area—the very, very lean. There's just not enough money in small farming anymore.

Caitlyn says we need to vote for the progressive candidates she's always pushing, like Bernie—her absolute favorite. They're looking out for the little guy, she tells me. But then you see these people you vote for get up to Jeff City or Washington, and they end up doing the same damn thing as everybody else, the same as Obama did to us. They end up forgetting their promises to break up the monopolies, 'cause those monopolies is suddenly writing checks for their next campaign. Oh sure, they'll send us some money in the way of government subsidies. But even those checks mostly go to the big guys, the guys who are whispering in their ears, who have the cash to spend in order to make more cash. They's also the ones who are the reason for all the regulations. You gotta have your manure pit fifty yards from here and your waste pond a hundred feet from there and your milk tanks have to be such-and-such temperature-controlled and your cows have to be fed such-and-such grain all because the big guys is the ones trying to cut corners. We've had our waste ponds and manure pits in the same area for damn near thirty years and there's never been an issue. But the big guys do something stupid, their waste ends up polluting some waterway, and suddenly, everybody has to change everything. It's not sensible! And even if they'll give you a loan to make the changes, what are the chances you're ever gonna pay that back when you're scraping by already? And it's not like most of us want a handout in the first place. We'd prefer to make money the old-fashioned way—good, hard work. But making sure farmers is pulling in a living wage ain't a sexy way to sell your campaign to the rest of America, not like gay rights and climate change and whether or not a woman is entitled to a legal abortion. So, of course, we get put on the back burner over and over, like little stupid whores who are promised the world by the men who come courting us, but who end up sucking dick in a seedy motel off the interstate for fifteen bucks a load and who are forgot the moment that load is shot.

If I sound angry about it, I am. And I suppose the anger could keep me going, but it's so fucking exhausting, it's literally eating me from the inside. And I'm tired of the hurt, the feeling like I ain't nothing to nobody. Fuck! I live in the goddamn woods, and I feel like the whole world hates me or is making fun of me or wishes I was dead for things I barely even understand. I don't know how Pop does it, except for the fact he has Mom, and well, it ain't always been this bad for him. There was good days. They might've been twenty years ago, but they weren't so awful when he was a young man and people respected him and saw him as an American hero for being a farmer. They was those days when I was stained clear up to my chin in walnut hull juice, and my best friend was my sister.

My Mom tells me I should get on social media to keep in touch with folks so I won't feel all alone like I do sometimes. And Lord knows, Mom loves her social media. She's always got the gossip on everybody who's moved, everybody who's got a new job or had a kid or got married or divorced. I've never been one much for computers or cell phones or any of that crap. It all feels so fake to me, especially when compared to the truth of a plump green leaf between your fingers, fresh river water on your face, the bawl of a newborn baby calf ringing in your ear. If you have to announce to the world that you've got cancer in a Facebook post, I think maybe there's something wrong with you much worse than cancer. Humans ain't made to operate economy size, no matter what anyone thinks or what we're told by the computer programs tracking our movements or the big companies that run our lives. Sure, we's complex creatures that can do amazing shit, but all the same, we're pretty damn simple. We're all running from pain and pursuing pleasure is what I read somewhere. And the tug of war we have with each other ain't nothing more than some people trying to bandage their hurt while others is trying to make themselves happy. And sometimes what makes one person happy is what hurts somebody else. And that's why humans are supposed to be decent and have morals. But what's decent and moral in this day and age, you may ask? 'Cause nowadays everybody thinks they're right, even murderers, rapists, thieves, and the like. Just get on social media, and you'll find somebody else somewhere's out in our world of eight billion people who feels the same stupid feelings as you. The way I see it, though, what's moral is real easy to tell from what's immoral. What's moral is what *don't* hurt anybody else. It's simple as that. And the moment you're hurting somebody else, well you've managed to get yourself outta step with what makes humans human. And maybe that's why I hate myself so much nowadays. 'Cause I feel like even if it ain't me specifically, it's people *like* me who have made the world so rotten awful. At least that's what they say. That's what Caitlyn says. Down with the patriarchy!

Kell's Walnuts is off AH Highway just outside of Raymondville. They've been there since before I was born. Priscilla and Gavin are the owners. Their kids, Travis, Ric, Mark, Amy, and Dean, work with them along with the sons' wives and Amy's husband and most of *their* kids. They're a Mormon family, so they's just about the nicest people you ever met despite the fact I know folks crack jokes about 'em behind their backs about how they's all inbred polygamists with five wives but the same mother-in-law. There was a time about fifteen years ago when an Assembly's of God church out of Rolla told its members to boycott all the Kell's selling stations around the state 'cause they said the Kells was bona fide heathens who didn't believe in the one true God. Unfortunately for the AG's, the only other place to take walnuts is all the way over in Springfield. So, that particular prohibition didn't last very long, especially 'cause so many families do it—get together a couple Saturdays and Sundays in the fall, pick walnuts, and take 'em into one of the Kell's selling stations to make a little cash.

While every other family business around the area seems to be getting steamrolled by some corporate outfit no one has ever heard of, the Kell's have made their little walnut shelling and distribution company into not just a well-respected enterprise, but a local attraction. People come from all over to visit the general store, walk through the black walnut tree orchards and have themselves some of Priscilla Kell's Famous Black Walnut Butter Brickle. Every spring, Fourth of July, and Labor Day Weekend, the Kell's host day-long events for locals and visitors alike with live music and BBQ, and of course, black walnut everything. From the highway, Kell's Walnuts still looks like a small family business too. But if you drive past the newly built general store, back behind it you'll find gleaming airplane-sized aluminum hangers for hulling, sorting, shelling, and packaging Southern Missouri Black Walnuts.

I pull into the area next to one of the first big buildings labeled "local drop-offs." Local walnuts aren't mixed with the Kell's orchard grown meats just in case the quality ain't up to snuff. Luckily, there ain't nobody else in line. So, I drive over a large grate into which all the walnuts from my trailer will be raked. Those walnuts will hit a conveyor belt below and move underground, over to the first building where they'll be hulled behind closed doors.

The oldest brother, whose name is "Travis" according to the tag on his black polo, walks up in a pair of starched Wranglers and new boots just as I step out of my truck. Travis is greying around his ears, but he has that perfect face all Mormons seem to have, fresh and kind-looking. He's followed by a young, blonde pony-tailed girl in overalls who looks like she ought to be in school, as well as a smiling blue and brown-eyed Australian Shepard.

"How's it going today?" Travis asks as though he recognizes me, but I'm not sure he actually does.

"Oh, you know. I'm gettin' along," I answer. "Brought you some walnuts."

"Fantastic. Let's see 'em," Travis says.

I make quick work of pulling the tarp back from the trailer to reveal my stash of treasure.

Travis looks over the walnuts with admiration. "These are some nice fruits."

"Yeah, my place is down by Paddy Creek. That holler over there is perfect for growin' walnut trees."

"We're doing seven cents a pound," Travis says, making sure I know the deal before he takes a single nut.

"Sounds good to me. How many pounds you think I got on here?" I ask.

"Guess we'll see."

I unlatch the back of the trailer and the walnuts start to topple down without any help. Then, the girl and Travis grab nearby rakes to push the rest of them onto the grate where the walnuts disappear way faster than they was found. In minutes, all that's left in the trailer bed is a slimy, brown goop that smells like moldy dirt. As soon as the last walnut is vanished, the girl takes off, and so does the dog, but Travis pulls out his cell phone.

"Looks like a thousand four hundred and twenty pounds," he says.

"You can tell that from lookin' at your phone?" I ask.

"Oh, yeah. It's all getting automated nowadays." He hits the phone a few times with his fingers and then looks back at me. "Ninety-nine dollars and forty cents. You can collect a check up at the general store. I already sent 'em the receipt."

"You guys sure seem to have it all done right," I say, admiring their gleaming buildings and new equipment everywhere.

"We're hanging in there," Travis responds. "But you know, end of the day, work is work, and some days it's easier than others."

"Yep, I sure *do* know."

"You guys have the dairy out off Z Highway, right?"

I realize maybe all along Travis *has* known who I am. Sure, we've met a few times, but still, I'm surprised. "That's right. Honeycutt Dairy," I say.

"How y'all doing?" he asks.

The way he asks it, you can tell he knows things have been hard for us. Or maybe he can see it in me, in the premature wrinkles on my face, the age of my truck, the wear of my boots. Suddenly, I feel tears welling up in my eyes like I'm gonna break down crying right then and there, but instead, I wave his question off and laugh out loud, "Oh, shoot! You know. Nobody ever got into dairyin' for the money." And I kick one of the tires on the trailer just to punctuate my joke and distract me from the tumult of emotion inside me.

"Yeah, I suppose you could say the same for guys selling walnuts," Travis laughs back.

This time when I look at Travis, I catch his eyes. And I wonder if deep inside he's feeling the pinch too. Now when I look around, I wonder how much money was borrowed to build all this up, and if he and his family lie awake at night anxious about how they's gonna pay it all back if something goes wrong, if all of a sudden some moron writes an article in some paper talking about how black walnuts ain't environmentally friendly food or gives you premature hair loss or is gonna kill everyone or Lord knows what else. I wonder if he's scared of what life would look like if suddenly the government were to go and add some new regulation to his business he ain't prepared for or decides to use 'em as pawns in one of those stupid trade wars that damn reality star president was so proud of. But Travis's grey eyes don't give nothing away. Instead, he smiles and offers, "We were friends with Chuck and Leanne Davis before they sold off their farm. I know it's been tough on all y'all as of late. Anyway, I hope you're doing better than most."

"Really appreciate you sayin' that," I smile. And I wonder if I should say something more. Travis seems like such a straightforward guy, and I wonder if I told him about how hard it's been if he'd go gossiping to everybody else about my problems. Or I wonder if maybe instead he'd offer me a beer and confide in me how his family has managed to grow their business like they have. Maybe he could offer me some hope, I think. Or maybe he's just like me, barely getting through the muck day by day by day.

Before I can make up my mind about saying something more, he gives me a nod, "Well, stop on by the general store up front and Mom or one of the girls will give you your check for the walnuts." And he walks back towards the big building all the hulled walnuts disappear into, and I suddenly remember, Mormons don't drink beer.

The general store at the front of the property is clad in natural wood siding and was made to look like it's ancient as any building in the county even though it's only a couple years old. It's where Priscilla sells walnut goods and other local crafts. There's a trio of swings that hang under a porch that spans the whole front of the building. I park in the paved lot and wander up the stairs to the open French doors where the smell of cinnamon and spice greet me from candles burning on a display table right up at the front of the store. Priscilla is sitting on a barstool behind a counter looking down through half-moon spectacles at a Bible in her lap when she hears me walk in. She peers over her glasses and smiles brightly. "Mr. Honeycutt, how are you doing today?"

Once again, the way my name is said, I wonder if she actually knows who I am or just knows my name 'cause of the mobile receipt Travis sent up.

"I'm alright," I smile back.

"You must've brought in quite a load of walnuts," she says, looking at a cash register where a couple receipts have just been printed out. "You want cash or a check?"

"Cash would be great. Thank you."

Before she opens the register, she walks over to a small display showcasing black walnut desserts. She grabs a glass cake stand and brings it over to me, lifting the lid so I can smell the cooked caramel scent of fresh fudge. "You like fudge?"

"Oh, yes, ma'am."

"Try one of these samples. Try two if you want," she winks.

I happily take a dime-size piece of fudge and put it in my mouth while she waits expectantly for my delight. And damn! I couldn't hide my appreciation if I tried. I put my hand over my mouth and exclaim, "Wow! That's so good."

"Made it this morning. I'll sell you a whole box for half off since you brought in walnuts."

I see the small, gift-wrapped box she's talking about, and I wonder how much it costs. It's probably expensive even with half off. "I'll be alright," I say.

"Suit yourself," she smiles, and she puts the cake plate back before returning to the till to grab the cash to pay me.

Over in the corner, I realize there's another person in the store, a young woman who's probably twenty years old or so. She's pretty. Dark brown hair. Freckles. No makeup. Great body. She's folding T-shirts. I suddenly realize I've been staring at her for far too long when I hear Priscilla close the register behind me. When I look back, she's holding out her hand with a hundred dollar bill in it.

"I don't have change," I shrug.

"That's fine, darling," she says.

"Thank you," I say, and I mean it. It's a damn good feeling to have a crisp, clean Benjamin in your hand, I'll tell you what. I almost hate to put it in my wallet, but I do. Then suddenly, the young woman folding T-shirts is now standing right beside me.

"Hi," she says quietly.

"Hey," I answer back.

"Did you want me to sort out the sizes or just fold everything nice?" the girl asks Priscilla, who has already returned to her barstool and Bible.

"No need to sort 'em. People dig through them regardless," Priscilla says.

I am not sure what kind of exit I'm supposed to make. So, I give the T-shirt gal, whose name tag reads "Daniella" a nod, then I look at Priscilla who is already back to reading her Bible as if I hadn't ever even showed up.

As I make for the door, I think about that fudge and scold myself for not buying a box. It was so damn tasty, and Mom woulda appreciated if I'd brought it home to her and Pop. Or maybe she would've been cross and told me I shouldn't have spent the money. Too expensive, she would have said. Then, I think about that young gal I saw folding T-shirts—Daniella. She looked so nice and sweet. Real genuine. The kinda girl a guy can only hope to marry. I bet the farm she ain't utterly and totally perplexing, I tell myself, not like so many of them women out there can be—not like that pharmacist whose name I won't even repeat. And for a moment, I imagine Daniella running out to my truck before I can exit the parking lot. She motions for me to roll down my dusty window.

She says I forgot something, and she holds up that little box of fudge. I tell her I didn't buy it, and she smiles at me that she knows. She brought it out to me so she could tell me her name. Then, she tells me, with the flirtiest smile I ever seen, that I outta come back and visit again soon. And I say, I will.

But the truth is, even if she came running out of the store right this moment and whispered all the beauty in the world right into my ear, I'd just look at her hollow and pretend like I wasn't interested from the cab of my dirty truck. And the truth is, I wouldn't be. Not really. Not now. Not ever again. 'Cause I'm a ruined man or maybe just a man in ruins. Still, I look in the rearview mirror as I pull out of the parking lot and turn onto the highway, and I wish so hard I could see her one last time, love and beauty—Daniella!

I'm not five minutes out from Kell's when I get a call from Miles. I know he's ringing me up to confirm about gigging tonight. He gets that I'm an honest broker, but he's also aware of how things happen on the farm and plans can change real quick. So, there's a bit of an understanding between us. This is more for Miles' sake than my own 'cause he likes to be reassured. I think this is 'cause he's had so many people let him down in his life.

Our friendship started back when we was both in grade school. Miles was the stud of the playground, and I figured being friends with him would help my little twelve-year-old self twofold: 1) Nobody picked on someone who was friends with Miles, and 2) Miles knew all the girls, and they knew him. However, for a young buck who looked like he could knock a grown man out cold, Miles was a clown and a tease, a walking, talking heart of gold. And the two of us hit it off real fast 'cause Miles liked to hunt and be out in nature, and well, with our farm big as it was, we had nature to spare.

Early on, we'd have weekends over at my folks' place, getting up early in the morning and taking our twenty-twos out to hunt squirrels and rabbits and explore the land. Mom and Pop were great about it too. Pop would usually let me slough off my chores, and Mom would give us Little Debbie treats for our backpacks. Maybe they liked it—us disappearing 'til sundown—'cause that meant we were out of their hair. And by then, Caitlyn was almost eighteen. So, she was usually holed up in her bedroom reading or writing college essays or swimming at her friend Amy's in-ground pool. Whatever the case, those were the most carefree days of my life. Miles and I hardly ever managed to shoot dinner, but we always succeeded in getting poison ivy, tick bites, mosquito welts, chiggers, leeches, and scratches all up and down our hides from encounters with fence lines, water holes, brush piles, and multi-flora rose. And though, I don't remember exactly what we talked about, we always seemed to have something to say to one another. Usually, our conversations had to do with the future and all our plans for it, how we was going to have this truck and that fishing boat or this girl and that farm. We talked a lot about trekking out to Montana—Big Sky Country—and driving around from one area to another, living off the land, hunting elk, swimming in glacier lakes, and drinking fresh water straight from mountaintops. The sun don't go down 'til midnight in the summer in Montana, Miles would always remind me as though that was the biggest selling point right there—endless days. Sometimes, we thought it'd be just about perfect to live on an island in a little hut somewhere in the middle of the Pacific Ocean. Whatever it was, we had intentions to do it all together. Of course, back then, we didn't know the limits that would come with growing up where we did, simple as we did, poor as we did. Back then, the idea of having the biggest dairy in all Missouri seemed like a right good plan, one that nothing and nobody could stop you from achieving. In the woods, we was God of everything, and the earth was our heaven.

Miles' mom, Charlene, disappeared the fall of our senior year one weekend when we was out deer hunting. She'd always been a little kooky, someone who was slightly frantic for no good reason. Their little craftsman in town was the most clean house I'd ever stepped foot in, everything in its place to a fault. Miles' clothes always smelt like fresh soap, and his hair was always cropped real close. But other than being a bit of a perfectionist, nothing seemed that off about Mrs. Snyder, at least not initially. She was smiling and accommodating if there was something Miles or I needed, including cigarettes. Miles had been smoking since he was thirteen. When I spent the night at his house, she'd let us stay up late watching TV and bake us an entire batch of oatmeal cookies all without the raisins because we both hated raisins. She even let us have girls over a few times, completely unchaperoned. Of course, after she went missing, I started recalling the bread crumbs she'd been dropping in plain sight of us boys that unfortunately would never lead us to her, but would at least help us understand why she went away. It was little things like she didn't have any real friends, at least none that Miles knew of. She was always changing jobs too, laid off from one and hired to another real inexplicable like. When I was over, she'd lock herself up in her bedroom for hours on end, then emerge again red-eyed and in a daze. And I'll never forget how she was always chewing gum. And when she wasn't, I could smell hot cinnamon on her breath. Miles told me that was the smell of rum. Mrs. Snyder liked to drink. We kept her absence a secret for a while because Miles confided in me this actually wasn't the first time she'd run off. Intermittently, throughout Miles' childhood, after his father divorced her, Mrs. Snyder would disappear. Usually, it was only for a few days or a week at most. And Miles knew the best thing he could do was keep quiet about it in order to *not* be turned over to the state or have his mom locked up. By the time she left in our senior year, though, Miles was old enough it didn't matter if his mom never showed her face again, and she didn't. Eventually, of course, people began asking where Charlene Snyder was, and after a while, Miles couldn't keep up the lies no more. For a hot second, there was an investigation by the sheriff, but that ended when Mrs. Snyder's trail went cold, last seen under a bridge with a bunch of meth heads down near Branson.

Despite how hurt I know he was by it, Miles never let on that he was bothered by the fact he'd pretty much been abandoned by both his mom and pop. And just to make sure he kept up appearances, there was always a smile on his face and a good joke in his back pocket. I offered to let him take Caitlyn's room when he had to move out of his house, but he refused. He got a part-time job at the grocery store unloading produce, and it paid enough he could afford a crumbly, ol' apartment on the filthy side of town that he kept as clean as his mom had kept their house.

I suppose my friendship with Miles would have gone the way of most high school friendships if either of us had left for college somewhere, but he got a job as a welder for a small farm equipment man-ufacturing company nearby, and I stayed on at the dairy helping Pop. We grew from boys to men side by side, hunting, fishing, gigging, and dreaming. Always dreaming, even though we both started to realize the older we got, the further out of reach those dreams became.

When Miles met Stacy—his now ex-wife—they had the type of chemistry that makes everybody else question why their own relation-ships ain't better. Miles and Stacy fit together like a worm and a hook. She was cute as a big-eyed fawn but with a tight curvy body, short-cropped chestnut hair, and a laugh that made a person feel like nothing in the world was really the matter. For a while, Miles wanted to include her in everything we was doing, which was actually nice. We was all around twenty-five or twenty-six at that time, and Stacy brightened up our same ol', same ol' routine, brought a female perspective into things, and in a way made it all seem new and exciting again.

Stacy was the first to admit she was a spoiled army brat. Her dad was a general or lieutenant or something over in Fort Leonard Wood, and while she'd initially gone to college to be a dancer, she'd ended up be-coming a nurse, which is how Miles met her—one night after he cut his foot open on a piece of broken beer bottle while we was down at the river swimming. Stacy worked at the county hospital in the ER, and she gave him her number "in case he had any questions about his pain meds." Well, the only question he had was if he could take her out to dinner sometime, which she agreed to without hesitation. Apparently, on their first date, they never made it to the restaurant. Instead, Stacy jumped Miles in his truck, and from that point on, they always had a post-sex glow about them. They even had sex when I was around. Not necessarily right in front of me, but they weren't exactly careful about it neither. And while I pretended not to know what they had slipped off to do, as we all hung out more and more, they became more and more loose about their escapades. Not that Stacy was ever shy. She was the first to take off her clothes to go for a swim if we was down at the river. And she didn't hold her tongue when there was something she wanted to say. If she was upset with Miles, she didn't try to keep it in. Oh, and she cursed like a farmer with a broke-down tractor. Every other word she said was four letters, which made Miles and me laugh, but also made me worry sometimes about taking Stacy around other people.

She climbed up on top of Miles one night when we was all sitting around a bonfire and pulled her top off. I looked at Miles unsure what I was supposed to do. He mumbled something to her about me being right there, but she just gave me a smile and told me to come closer. Of course, I didn't move a muscle. Hell, I'm not sure I even blinked. Neither did Miles. Stacy took off her pants next, and then bent over right in front of me so I could see all that beautiful pink glistening between her legs. Then, she pulled Miles' pants off him and got up on his dick, riding him reverse cowgirl so she was facing me, touching herself, and letting her little titties jiggle up and down. The way she looked at me, I knew she wanted me to want her. And well, I gotta tell you, I had a boner the size of Texas, but I also thought I might pass out from anxiety, I was so damn nervous about the whole situation. After a few minutes, they both came hard, then put their clothes back on as though nothing out of the ordinary just happened. And for the longest time, I hugged myself and stared at the fire while they cuddled and did the same. When I finally did lock eyes with Miles, he just gave me a sly grin, and I knew everything was good. And dammit all if I didn't wish I woulda let go and touched Stacy like she wanted me to like I'm pretty sure Miles was okay with. I promised myself the next time the opportunity arose, I'd partake in the hedonism, but it never did. Stacy got pregnant, and well, that changed everything.

I remember Miles calling me dead of night to tell me Stacy had missed her period, and they'd gone through three test strips that all flashed the same positive sign. Stacy was adamant she didn't want a baby. Miles said he didn't neither. But I could tell there was hesitation on his part, probably 'cause the idea of taking Stacy for an abortion created a fear in him that somehow he was behaving like his parents, skirting duty, abandoning his kid. Still, they made the appointment to go do it. But apparently, when they got into the room, Stacy changed her mind. And I'm pretty sure Miles was relieved. Then in two months' time, they was married. Everybody knew the reason for their quick nuptials was that Stacy was preggers. But honestly, it didn't matter what the reason was. End of the day, those two seemed perfect for each other.

Their first baby was a little girl, named Kayla. Their second came in quick succession and was named Maya. Miles was a great dad. I mean, he was there for those little girls, working three times as hard to make sure they had everything they needed and wanted. Hell, I barely even saw him for a couple years he was so busy taking care of his little family. Sure, we'd talk on the phone once in a while or run into each other out and about, but otherwise, his whole life was Stacy and those two babies. And maybe that's why Stacy ended up cheating on him 'cause he started to run ragged, let himself go. Truth is, he was so busy providing for his family that he wasn't actually around to attend to their other needs. Or maybe this was the way it was always going to be, Stacy—the spoiled army brat—taking whatever she wanted no matter how it might effect anyone else. And maybe things still woulda been okay between 'em if the affair Stacy got herself in hadn't been with a Black woman named Fantasia who worked the cash register at a filling station off the interstate in Cabool. According to Miles, Fantasia was a butch lesbian with cornrows like a prison inmate, and she was determined to keep Stacy as her own. Miles said Stacy told him more than once how she might be bisexual, but it wasn't until he showed up home one night and everything was packed up and gone that he knew her relationship with Fantasia was more than just a phase.

Suddenly, Miles was back in my life. Every free minute he had, he was calling me so I could talk him down off the ledge he'd found himself out on. Poor fucking guy. I begged Stacy to be gentle on him, but she just cursed me out when I tried to talk to her. The divorce was worse than a brawl between two rabid opossums, and Miles didn't do himself any favors when he lost his job and showed up at the courthouse drunk out of his mind. He basically squandered all rights to his girls right then and there and was still gonna have to work himself to the bone to pay the alimony the judge handed down to Stacy. No wonder he ended up in the hospital one night with alcohol poisoning. I mean, shit.

I did my best to be there for him through everything, but I can't take credit for his survival. He was the one who found an AA group and started attending regularly. He was the one who started showing up every Sunday for services at church. He was the one who wrote letters of apology to his old employers and the judge and Stacy and the kids and even Fantasia. When he tried to apologize to me, I wouldn't hear it. That's what friends are for, right, the tough times and the good times? And we all know the truth; you don't get one without the other. But Miles and I were more than friends. At this point, I'd known him longer than I'd not known him—almost twenty years. He was my brother.

"Hey," I answer my cell phone.

On the other end of the line, Miles clears his throat. Then I hear him take a pull on a cigarette; that's the one bad habit he can't seem to kick. "How's it goin'?" he asks.

"Just dropped off a trailer full of walnuts over at Kell's."

"How much they give you for 'em?"

"Seven cents a pound."

"That's good."

"Yeah, came out to about a hundred bucks."

"Guess I don't feel so bad askin' you to pick up propane for the fry cooker tonight, then," Miles says, coughing and clearing his throat. "I'll be late if I try to get into town to find some after work."

"Glad you told me now. I'll pick up a tank on my way back to the farm."

"You hear about Hatcher Mings' folks?"

"Yeah. There anymore news?"

"Don't think Rhett's gonna make it is what I heard, and even if he does, he'll probably be a vegetable."

"Tough fuckin' break, man."

"That's what Hatcher's girlfriend Rhonda told somebody who told a guy I work with."

"I should send him a text, I suppose."

"Yeah, me too. Ain't seen the guy in forever, though." Miles clears his throat again.

"Weather is supposed to be real good tonight," I say, changing the subject.

"Anything will beat last time and all that sleet that started up," Miles says. "Couldn't see a goddamned thing," he laughs.

"Yeah, there's somethin' about giggin' frozen fish that just don't feel quite as sportin'," I smile.

Miles is silent. Then, he coughs and says, "Can't imagine what he must be goin' through, though. And if he loses them both? Fuck."

I know Miles is talking about Hatcher's folks, and given his background of losing the people he loves, I'm sure what's going on with the Mings' family bothers him right good.

"Well, I oughta get goin'," I say, even though I don't got a thing to get going for.

"Alright. I appreciate you grabbin' the propane," he tells me.

"See ya in a bit."

"See ya then."

Once I'm off the phone, I feel guilty for hanging up, for not talking Miles off the Mings' tragedy like I know he needed. He'll spiral about that like a fucking tornado all afternoon. And suddenly, I'm anxious again 'cause the truth is I'm about to nuke Miles' life in a way nobody ever has. That's why I had to wait until after gigging tonight to say goodbye to this world. 'Cause I gotta watch out for Miles. I gotta soften the blow that's coming. I ain't telling him what I'm gonna do 'cause he'd probably try and stop me somehow. Still, I'm gonna make sure he understands my leaving has nothing to do with him. If anything, he's been a salve on the harsh reality of my world, the only real light in my slowly darkening life. And the sad thing is, he won't even hate me for doing what I'm gonna do, for abandoning him just like everybody else has.

No, he'll blame himself. He'll believe it's all his fault totally and completely like somehow he's the guilty one, not me.

Tonight will be wonderful, though, I tell myself. I'm gonna end things on a high note with Miles. Even though I wish I could just end everything now, I'm gonna wait. I'm gonna do this right, so I don't leave some mess for everybody else to clean up, so everybody knows I did what I did 'cause I'm selfish—not because of them—and there's nothing they coulda done to change it.

By the time I arrive in Licking, I'm starved. So, I leave the main road that runs past the new Kum & Go, Dollar General, KFC, and Mc-Donald's and head for the ol' main street, which is mostly abandoned and boarded up now, the sidewalks all cracked and sprouting weeds. When I was a kid, this was the place to be, this place that's now all crumbling brick buildings and splintering wood signs. Through the years different folks have tried to revitalize downtown, moving into some shop, painting, updating, decorating. But just one person can't save an old main street on their own. Sure, some little coffee shop or florist is popular for a few months, but eventually, people get tired of going to the same place, especially if it's out of the way, there ain't other shopping around, and it costs more than what they can get at Walmart, a fast-food drive-thru, or delivered online.

At the tail end of main street is the last place still standing in downtown, Wade's filling station and garage. Unlike all the other mom-and-pop businesses that've vanished, Wade's is still carrying the torch of days past underneath all the rust and dirt that's tried to eat it alive. Oris and Patty Wade have kept their place going even after they was informed by the powers that be they'd have to spend half their savings to put in new gas tanks in accordance with EPA regulations, even after they was told they'd have to dispose of tires for twice the amount of money they previously did, even after they was forced to buy new no-spill gas pumps and update all their electrical panels and apply for a specialty food license if Patty wanted to sell baked goods out of the filling station store. And I suppose that's the only upside to the hell they've been put through to stay in business, instead of selling her baked goods on the sly out of the filling station, she opened a small diner next door.

I pull into the gravel parking lot of Patty's Diner. It's a small lot, but luckily empty, being as I have the trailer hitched on my truck. The John Deere green building where Patty serves up all kinds of fixings was a shack of a house before the Wade's decided to scrap the rooms inside and turn it into a shack of a restaurant. As such, it ain't a particularly sought-after destination. There's no real decor to speak of, just a bunch of picnic tables covered in checkered plastic table cloths sitting haphazard on concrete floors inside and out. Most of the fixings aren't exactly healthy, but *it is* pretty damn tasty. Also, it's a helluva lot cheaper than Sonic or McDonald's for the same amount of grease and sugar. So, if you're willing to go a little out of your way, it's a right good experience. A lot of us farmers around the area like to congregate at Patty's to shoot the shit over a fifty cent cup of joe or a dollar and fifty cent piece of pie. The place looks dead this afternoon, but I don't think much of it until I reach the locked front door where a handwritten sign has been posted on the window: "Closed Until Furthur Notice!!" For a moment, I gotta be honest, I can't quite comprehend what I'm reading. Then, I hear a whistle from behind me and see the roly-poly of a man that is Oris Wade, sixties and bald as a light bulb, lumbering out from the mechanic shop in a heavily soiled pair of overalls. He's wiping his flushed red face with a dirty shop cloth.

I immediately head his direction. "Patty alright?" I ask.

"She's fine, over in Rolla."

"Sign says, 'Closed until further notice.' How long she gon' be over there?"

Oris wipes his face again and chuckles, rocking back and forth on his heels. "Well, truth is, we just can't afford to keep the diner open no more. So, she's started herself a job at Walmart."

I remove my cap and run my hand through my hair, completely flummoxed. "What do you mean, you can't afford to keep the diner open no more?"

"Just what I said. It was never makin' much money to begin with, but here recently, it's just become more work than it's worth." Oris shrugs, and he spits on the ground. "Last few months, things have been so slow, Patty's done thrown out food. And dammit all if she weren't workin' mornin', noon, and night for pennies to begin with. So, she told me she was through, and I agreed with her. Last week there was two days straight nobody came in at all."

"You kiddin' me? You got people in there all the time. Dan and Cade McClury. Mike and Austin and Sally and their little one. Shane and Kayla Wright. I mean, that's crazy—plenty o' folks is comin' in."

Oris smiles and spits again. "I know it's crazy. Damn straight it's crazy. But it's the truth. We's too far off the main drag now, and people...well, they've just plumb forgot about us."

I look back at the diner, and to be honest, I'm kinda pissed. I mean, I've been coming to that damn diner since the day it opened. Then, I look back at Oris, and suddenly, I can tell despite his smile, his face is redder than usual and his eyes are all broken out like he's been crying. "I'm sorry," I offer.

"She's workin' the clothing department, foldin' shirts, openin' dressin' rooms, and gettin' different sizes for people. She's only been doin' it a couple days, but she says it's real nice for the most part. And even if the pay ain't much, at least it's gonna be regular."

"Yeah, that's a nice Walmart," I say, but the truth is, it ain't. Walmart has moved in all over the place around here, stealing business from mom-and-pop shops until every last one has shuttered their doors. Then, Walmart has the gall to offer all them moms and pops work for even less money than they was making working for themselves. After a few years, with no competition, of course, those gleaming, glistening crayon blue stores full of promise and hope turn to shit—dirty floors, broken shelves, cheap everything. Dollar General does the same thing, only smaller and shittier. And for some reason, people don't have the sense to say, "No." Actually, they do have the sense, but they can't help themselves. They see something sparkly and shiny and new around here, and they just have to drop by. And can you blame 'em? Not much new happens around these parts. Then, of course, all the prices is so cheap, and well, it's all so convenient they show up again and again. Next thing you know, they's hooked like they was on drugs or something. Forget quality. Forget healthy. Forget supporting your own damn town and your own goddamned people, you want your fucking bleach for ninety-nine cents a gallon and your food frozen solid as a brick and your milk—well, don't even get me started on that. And who am I to blame 'em? I'm one of 'em. Beggars can't be choosers, right?

"I can still patch tires, put on brake pads, or install a new muffler, if you need it," Oris smiles. "And we still got gas. Course, I don't know how much longer I'll be doin' all this either. You know my back is shot. Takes me a handful of aspirin and twice as long as it once did to change even one oil pan. Truth be told, I'm just holdin' out 'til my social security kicks in."

I look over at my truck, but for as run down as it is, it currently seems to be working just fine. "I don't know what I'll do without some of Patty's peach pie or her famous chicken fried steak," I say.

"Well, I'll tell her you stopped in. Maybe she can make you somethin' special. I'm sure she wouldn't mind."

"Oh, gosh. Well, I'll pay her good money for it," I laugh. And I think about that fudge I passed up earlier at Kell's.

"You're a youngin', Calem. You have any clue what happened?" Oris asks.

"What do ya mean?"

"I mean, how'd we all get to this place? One day we're sittin' here doin' good, things is glorious as heaven, and the next day it's turned all to hell. People used to love this place. We was the envy of them yuppies. They'd drive out here from all over to watch the leaves change color in the fall, to breathe in the fresh air, to walk down main street and talk about how we all got it right. Now, they just drive on through faster and faster and faster, except when they need to take a piss or a shit. Where they all goin'? What're they all doin'? What's out there that's so much better than what we got here? I can't figure it out."

"Oh, Mr. Wade, this place is still heaven alright. It's just the devil has done his best runnin' out all the angels."

"Well, it's workin'. Makes me glad I'm almost gone anyways. I can't even imagine bein' a youngin' like you. I suppose you'll be around to see it, when they smash what's left of these ruins down and build a factory to make more shit for city folk." Oris shakes his head, spits, "Oh Calem, I'm sorry. I sound like an ol' fuddy-dud. I sound like my wife." He laughs at this, his belly jiggling under his overalls.

I smile too. "We're all fuddy-duds to them folks out there. Don't you worry none. Personally, I'm proud of bein' a fuddy-dud."

Oris don't laugh at my joke, though. He looks up at the sun is as though he's expecting it to fall out of the sky next. "You think if we'd done it different somehow things could've turned out another way?"

I look up too, but seeing the sun has already passed its zenith for the day, makes my stomach crawl. With the setting of the sun, comes the real terror—the Night Call that makes a person sweat, makes you curl up in your sheets asking God to take it all away. But he don't. The pains in your belly tell you the truth, and the message is one you wouldn't wish on your greatest enemy—the message of you mean nothing, you piece of shit. The world is a better place without you in it 'cause you's everything that's wrong with the world. They plumb decided that for you, whoever the fuck they is. I try to forget what's coming. I clench my jaw and hold my insides tight.

"Sure, things coulda turned out another way," I say. "But we didn't do things different. We did 'em the way they are. And besides, the truth is, things have been done to us we ain't chosen, by folks we don't know, who ain't interested in who we are, who—like you said—consider us only to take a piss or a shit."

Oris nods. "They say we's backwards. Well, we didn't start out that way, you know. Maybe it's them who's got it all turned around. What do you reckon?"

I smile, "You may very well be right."

"Course, I suppose you can't turn the Titanic, can you? Not now," Oris sighs.

"No," I reply.

"So, we's all just screwed, huh? Every last one of us."

"Unless there's a miracle," I say.

"Only miracle I'm aware of is Patty's peach pie," Oris smiles. "I'll make sure she knows you stopped in. And I'll make sure she bakes one up for you too. You've always been a good kid, Calem. A real good kid. Maybe you'll figure it out, what the rest of us ain't been able to."

Oris looks me in the eyes, and I know he means what he says—that I might be some sorta savior, and it's almost terrifying. I ain't no God. I ain't no great hope. Who does he think he's looking at? Still, I smile back. "Well, good to see you, Mr. Wade. You take care, now, ya hear?"

"You too," he says.

Then, Oris turns back to his mechanic shop, and I turn and head back to my truck. But I can't shake his words to me about figuring it all out. Don't he know of all people, I've got it figured the least? I ain't anyone who can do something. All the people who could do something have left these parts, like my sister Caitlyn. She was the one with the good grades and the smarts, and even *she* has given up on us, or maybe we gave up on her. Either way, I start up my truck and pull out of the parking lot. I'm hungry as hell, so I gotta get something to eat. I think I'll swing by McDonald's or Hardee's or Sonic. That will be quick and cheap. Then, I kick myself for being another one of those people that's feeding the beasts—the big businesses that are consolidating all the power, that are turning the whole damn world into an endless conveyor belt of meaninglessness. We've become the fucking cows. We stand around chewing our cud, waiting to be told what to do, while the big businesses decide what they want us to eat, what they want us to see, what they want us to feel. All the while, they's lining us up, sucking the very lifeblood right out of us, making our lives less worthwhile with each generation, domesticating us for use like fucking livestock. Trust me, I know. Maybe that's the natural order of things, one or two apex predators in charge of the rest of the farm, and if you ain't in charge, then fall in line, buddy, you is just shit out of luck.

Suddenly, I ain't hungry no more. I tell myself instead of eating I need to go to the bank. That's next on my list at any rate. I've been trying not to think about what a joy it's gonna be telling them assholes how I only got half the mortgage I owe, even with the Benjamin in my wallet. They'll look at me like I'm some sort of leach, and even if I know I'm not, I'll feel like I am. But fuck it. The truth is what the truth is. As for eating, I'll wait until I get back to the farm. Mom will have something I can toss in my belly with a little coffee. Then, tonight I'll have some fried hogsuckers fresh out of the crick with Miles. And then, before the Night Call begins in earnest, I'll shut it up right quick. I'll get off this damn conveyor belt. I'll escape the herd. Nobody is gonna wrangle me up no more. I'm gon' be free.

Mom and Pop helped me put up the down payment for my raggedy ol' farmhouse eight years ago when they had that cash on hand from my grandpa passing. My pop said giving me a leg up was the least they could do. I'd been working at the dairy for next to nothing for about as long as either of us could remember. He knew there was no way I'd be able to save up enough otherwise. I'll admit, it was nice getting those keys for my own homestead. It was a few miles down the road from Mom and Pop, though in backwoods terms we was practically living on top of each other. The land was twenty acres of pasture and forest up a hill from a crick with a pond and a walnut grove. The building was a three bedroom, one bathroom, two-story traditional with wooden floors, a cast-iron claw-footed tub, a wraparound front porch, and a falling-apart chicken coop and shed. It had belonged to two families before I bought it, including the elderly husband and wife who died in it from gas poisoning ten years prior. Yes sir, I felt like a real adult with those tiny pieces of metal jangling in my pocket, reminding me a small piece of earth now belonged to me—all to me. And unless there was some unforeseeable circumstance completely out of my control, no one could ever take it away.

When I first moved in, I only had the little bit of furniture Mom had gave me, my old bed and mattress, nightstand, and dresser, which were, of course, hand-me-downs from her mom. But back then, I didn't mind the hollow quietness of all the empty rooms at night. Sometimes, after milking, I'd get home and strip off all my dirty clothes and lay naked, splayed out on my bed, just staring up at the ceiling thinking about everything and nothing. It felt like the first time in my life I actually could think uninterrupted. I started looking forward to those times truly and utterly alone, letting my mind wander where it might. When I was left undisturbed, my thoughts was like wild mushrooms, silently growing up and out of a forest floor, bigger and bigger, expanding like a flooded crick with tributaries, filling in spaces here and there no one's ever seen. There's nothing quite like being swept away by your thoughts, following 'em every which way down this road and that. There are so many solutions to all the mysteries of the universe inside of you, you can't even imagine until you're there in the quiet all alone and you see 'em like signs on an otherwise abandoned dirt road. They feed you honesty if you listen to 'em good enough. They offer you hope and happiness. They warn you of dangers to come and obstacles to watch out for. Following my random thoughts was where I figured out what was making my truck's engine smoke and how to fend off those damn deer that was eating up Mom's garden, and why some girl had broken things off with me for what felt like no good reason. And yes, sometimes my thinking would arouse me, especially when I was naked and images of certain women floated through my mind. I suppose I should be ashamed of myself. I would lay there masturbating on and off for hours thinking of women I wanted to be with, how we'd meet and talk, and they'd let me take their bodies and do with them as I pleased. In my mind, those women could be anyone, actresses on TV, the Asian waitress at the Chinese restaurant in town, or even Miles' wife Stacy. They liked me, these women. They all got me, my jokes, my way of thinking, the way I liked to be touched. I'd get myself close to coming, and then I'd stop just to make myself even more eager to come, to prolong the fantasies of romance that I knew I'd never taste in real life. Sure, playing with myself was carnal. But just thinking for the hours that I did would have been *el scandalo* to most folks. For me, it was wondrous. If the body is safe, the mind can play, and I let it. Of course, as I learned later, a well-primed mind can also turn against you. A healthy brain flush with the power of unlimited imagination can become a sword of extreme fright and absolute terror, given the right outside pressures.

Despite being new to me, the house was constantly reminding me how old it was. In the spring, it leaked 'cause the roof needed patched. In the fall, it groaned as the wind whistled right through all the cracks in the windows and doors. In the summer, it sagged with the heat, and in the winter, it froze solid as a block of ice. There was no insulation between the clapboard siding outside and the plaster walls inside, so most of the time the whole place seemed to be made out of nothing more than a deck of cards, which was especially apparent when you heard lightning striking, birds chirping, insects thrumming, and wild animals calling. It sounded like they was all right inside the house with you. For obvious reasons, I repaired what needed tending to like the leaky gas pipes that had done in the previous tenants, but otherwise, I mostly left the house alone. And aside from Mandy cleaning it up with me that one time she came over, I liked all the dust and dirt, the bruises and scars of a place well lived in. Besides, I didn't have much money to do things up anyway 'cause I was now spending all my extra on that damn mortgage payment. So, things was gonna have to stay the way they were, at least for the time being. As for the other boarders, the carpenter ants, wolf spiders, termites, mice, and bats, I'm sure I coulda done something about them too, run 'em out and kept 'em out with enough attention, but who cared? The way I saw it when I took ownership of 1 Little Creek Road, they all became my responsibility, and I needed to treat 'em with the care of a respectful proprietor. I weren't no asshole from the city who needed everything sanitized least I touch a germ. No, we could all live in peace together, the invertebrates and vertebrates alike. Besides, I liked watching the critters go about their work. They reminded me of me, always hunting, eating, building, and well—when they was lucky—fucking.

I'll never forget the day I signed the paperwork to buy my house. I'd darkened the door of InterCounty Bank plenty of times as a kid with my parents, then again as a teenager when I opened my first savings and checking accounts. Truth be told, I used to love that place. The building was over a hundred years old, and she'd aged better than anything else in the county. The old hardwood floors were slick and shiny with years of lacquer, and there was brass bars that fell from the ceilings all the way down to the marble counters the tellers stood behind, making 'em seem like they worked in some sort of exotic birdcage. On display next to a row of chairs by the front window was the old vault, a chunk of metal the size of an elephant's belly, with a spindle that looked like it could steer a ship and doors gaping open so you could peek inside. Unfortunately, the bank was robbed three times before I ever even graduated high school, so by the time I bought my house, InterCounty had torn the old place down and built a new, more secured one. The new bank was an ugly, dark brick block building that had thick glass on the windows and security cameras everywhere. There was baby blue carpet on the floors and bulletproof glass protecting the tellers behind their new Formica counters. Gone was the old vault too. Now, there was just overstuffed chairs in the lobby along with fake silk flowers. Also lost with the old place, was the casual ease of everyone who worked there. Just like the new, stuffy building, all the InterCounty employees had become stiff overnight as well. Apparently, the president of the bank, Mr. Green, was the instigator of these changes 'cause he was hoping to expand the bank with more branches around the tristate area. As I sat in his office waiting to sign the paperwork they'd put together for me, I remembered wishing the bank looked like it used to, less formal, less institutional. My mouth was dry and my hands were slick with sweat from my nerves. And it didn't help that InterCounty now seemed so sterile and impersonal. Maybe this was the way they wanted it though, fake smiles and artificial air pumped into the place, so you'd know they weren't like you. They was much, much better.

Mr. Green had been friends with my pop since I could remember, and he was happy to take my business, especially 'cause Pop was right there with me, forking over the down payment and co-signing the pile of loan docs they sat in front of us that was so tall if they was a stack of pancakes they woulda made you thrown right up. Seriously, they've thought of everything in that damn paperwork, so as to make you—the borrower—liable for practically breathing, and them—the lender—responsible for nothing more than the paper and pen they give you to sign away your life. Page after page. Signature after signature. Before it's all over, they take your damn fingerprint and everything like if you miss a payment, they ain't just gonna foreclose on your ass, they's sending your ass to jail! Pop assured me I had nothing to worry about. The mortgage was less than some people's car payments. But Pop had taken out dozens of loans by that time, small loans and big to get the farm running and keep it running. He was old hat to signing on the dotted line. I was barely twenty-six, and any number with more than one zero behind it impressed the hell out of me—not to mention a number with five zeros. Still, I rubbed my sweaty palms on my jeans after it was all over, smiled real nice, and shook everybody's hands like I knew what I'd done.

And that's why I suppose you'd be right to blame me for the pickle I've found myself in now, unable to pay my damn bills. But how could I know what the future would hold? How could I know about Obama cutting out whole milk from school programs, Big AG slowly shutting us little guys down with their piggy banks up in D.C., that fucking reality star president starting a trade war he had no clue how to win, or how Covid-19, the damn China virus—*Yes, that's what it is! Thank you very much for eating raccoons and bats, you fucking assholes!*—would wreck the U.S. economy and force us to drain thousands of gallons of milk into our goddamn manure lagoons? I never went to college or even trade school, and I won't say graduating from high school around here is some incredible feat. I ain't some brilliant mind, but I also ain't just some dumb hick. I understand the people around here and life around here in ways somebody with twenty college degrees never could. I know what the shape of a cloud and the moisture in the air says about the coming weather without ever turning on the TV. I know when it's time to cut hay for baling or when to move the cows so they don't overgraze a pasture. I understand heifers better than most vets. I see the way they walk and the clarity in their eyes and know if they's down or if they's feeling good and how that means they're gonna behave one day to the next. I got life know-how you can't learn except one way—living. Also, I know how to stretch a penny further than any yahoo on Wall Street could even imagine, and I have! Money may mean a lot to city slickers, but it means even more to us country folk 'cause, well, here it's especially hard to come by. Here, you can be the biggest idiot in the world and if you got money, we'll roll out the red carpet for you like you is king, even if we don't like you. All you have to do is show up driving a fancy truck or wearing a nice pair of cowboy boots and folks will turn a blind eye to your character or your morals. They'll call you a friend 'cause they think if you have money that makes you worth something, and by default, makes them worth something. But I was hardly worth anything to anybody before, and I'm worth even less now.

So yeah, go ahead and blame me. Blame all us hicks out here for our shortsighted judgement, for not being more enlightened. Just understand, our way of life depends on calculations made on the fly in order to survive the ever-changing terrain we call home. And most of the time we all feel so far removed from the lives we are told on TV and movies that we're supposed to be living, it's easy to lose focus of anything other than getting a leg up anyway you think you can. And no, we don't always understand all the big words and concepts thrown at us from people who say they know better. But if you've spent more money on a college degree than most people around here will ever make in two lifetimes, fuck you if you got all the answers, but you don't know how to translate them into a language *we* can understand! Yes, I'm talking about liberals in particular. Fuck you—*especially you!* Your cities is overrun with garbage and shitty air and all kinds of crime and you want to tell me how you can make *my* life better? Get your heads out of your goddamned assholes and clean up your own spilled sewage before you come and try to tell me how to clean up mine! And no, that don't mean I think idiot conservatives is any better. We all know they's stupid as shit too and corrupt as can be. I ain't even sure how they walk upright, they is so damn spineless most of the time. But they say they believe in Jesus and guns and the American flag, and well, I guess that's at least something.

I sound like I'm sloughing off responsibility for how bad things have got for me and so many of the folks around me, and maybe I am. But I honestly don't know what to do. I don't want to follow all the damn lemmings off the fucking cliff, but the fact may be that the cliff is crumbling beneath us. Truth is, I'm sick—literally sick to my stomach about feeling so fucking helpless. I hate that I'm circling the drain. When I started having the pains in my gut back last year after that incident with the crazy pharmacist, I knew they was 'cause I saw the end coming at me, just like you see the end coming in a bad movie. Something about that incident woke me up to the reality I was living in. And once you see reality, there's nothing you can do to unsee it. Oh sure, I tried to think my way out of the predicament I found myself in. I'd lay there for hours on my bed with all my insect friends thinking of a better way. But unlike times past, the answers didn't come. I turned off FOX news and listened to MSNBC like my sister told me to. I even tried to read one of the national papers instead of listening to the local gossip chain, but that only made me realize even more there ain't no future for a straight, white guy with no skills other than working a farm. So, no matter how much I tried to think it out, I couldn't find an answer that was any better than the one I've come up with—leaving this world. I mean, I hate that I hate my life. Fact is, I chose the life I have. I don't want anything else. But the life I have has dried up faster than a cow's teats after too much milking. And the more I've realized that the sicker I've got, pains shooting up from my feet, straight through my stomach to my head, doubling me over. No sooner do I eat, than most of the time, I vomit it up or shit it all out again. It's embarrassing. It's disgusting. And goddammit, I'm scared!

Going to see my doctor up in Springfield is what sealed the deal for me, though. That's what really spelled the end. I didn't tell Mom and Pop what I was doing on those days I took off beginning of the year. I'd make up excuses about needing to repair something in the house or meeting up with Miles to go fishing. I didn't want 'em to worry. And truthfully, at first, I thought I was lucky 'cause I had that Obamacare. But dammit all if the deductible wasn't so fucking high having insurance barely seemed to matter. Still, I guess it was something. I mean those bills were crazy expensive, and I only paid a fraction of what they went for. Dr. Kelly, who I'd been going to since I was a teenager, ran tests on everything from my blood to my feces, and when none of those tests showed any problems, he sent me through an MRI machine that terrified the bejesus out of me. Nothing like being a six-foot, two-inch guy shoved into a tiny tube that buzzes so loud you can't hear yourself speak—at least not until you're yelling your head off and punching the tiny button they give you, screaming at them to get you out otherwise you swear your heart is gonna explode outta your chest!

In the end, Dr. Kelly couldn't find nothing wrong. So, he suggested I stop drinking coffee, eat less fried foods, and start taking antacids when I felt queasy. He also gave me the number of a shrink he wanted me to talk to. But paying a hundred bucks an hour to tell all my problems to a city slicker I didn't know from Adam sounded a bit ridiculous. Add to that the fact I'd already spent my entire life savings only to be told my very real pain was all in my head, and well, I figured I'd been through enough. So, I stopped thinking. That's what you do at a certain point. You stop thinking, and you just get through, day by day by day.

It's just as I pull into the InterCounty Bank parking lot, I feel that pain in my belly that apparently has no known cause. And when I step out of my truck, I know I have mere seconds before diarrhea will come exploding out of me. I close my eyes and head for the front door of the bank. I know there's a bathroom just off the lobby. I can only hope no one sees me rush in like a madman, face all scrunched up in agony. But damn my luck if there ain't the bank president himself, Mr. Green, leaned against the counter in front of one of the tellers. He straightens right up when I walk in.

"Mr. Honeycutt. Good afternoon," he says.

"I'm just gonna use your restroom real quick," I say, and I head for the bathroom door without waiting for Mr. Green's response.

Luckily, the door is unlocked, and no one is inside. So, I make like a fucking bandit, slam shut that door behind me and lock it tight. Then, I rip my pants down and sit on the toilet just as my rear end explodes into the bowl loud enough I know they heard it out front. And I want to die. I literally just want to disappear from the world. I don't want to deal with the mess anymore. I don't want to deal with the pain. Then suddenly out of nowhere, I sob out loud like a fucking dog that knows it's being put down. Before the second sob can come out, I clamp my palms over my mouth and cry into my own damn hands like a little baby. Then, I lean my head against the cool tile wall, and I tell myself it's almost over. This is the last day you have to go through this.

When we was kids Caitlyn was the one who gave Mom and Pop hell, not me. There was a wild streak in her that would spontaneously spark-to, like a bolt of lightning. Mom would shake her head never surprised but always disappointed when Caitlyn inevitably rebelled against some long-standing rule she and Pop had laid out for us kids, like church clothes on a bed. The year I was born—when Caitlyn was only five—she refused to stay inside if there was snow on the ground. It could be ten below zero, and she'd manage to slip out the door when Mom and Pop weren't looking to make snow angels in nothing more than a nightgown and bare feet. Even when she got pneumonia, hacking and coughing, she tried her best to escape. It got to the point Mom and Pop started locking her up in her own bedroom at night, 'causing her to scream her head off until she fell asleep. Apparently, Mom started to believe Caitlyn was somehow brain damaged, and the only bright spot of those tender years was the fact I was an easy-going baby who needed nothing more than a diaper change and a bottle in my mouth to keep me happy. Otherwise, Mom swore to us later, she would have had a total nervous breakdown before winter was over that year.

When she turned eight, Caitlyn decided she was going to stop Mom and Pop from dairying 'cause she found out what happened when a boy calf was born on a dairy farm—basically, they was sent off to make someone somewhere a nice steak or burger. But no matter how Mom and Pop tried to assure her the way they were running the farm was the way things had been done for thousands of years, Caitlyn refused to listen. At first, she tried escaping one night with all the boy calves in tow, which proved to be futile given that bovines are not exactly known for following orders, especially the little ones. Then, she tore apart the swings on our swing set and used the flimsy, little aluminum chains to shackle herself to the calves' fences when the time came to send them off to the sale barn—a matter with which she tried her best to involve me. Finally, when she realized she was fighting a losing battle all by herself, she looked up the number for PETA, called them and begged them to come out and do an investigation of the farm. Well, when someone did show up with a video camera and questions, Pop just about lost his shit, the sheriff was telephoned, curse words were said, I'll never forget, and Caitlyn hid out in her room for almost a month and didn't speak to Pop for almost half a year.

By the time she was ten, Caitlyn was a full-on vegan. When she turned twelve, all the commotion was about going to church and how bad religion was for you. When she was fourteen, it was over boys. When she was sixteen, it was over where she planned to go to college. When she was eighteen, she couldn't stop going on about gay rights. Then, it was climate change. Then, it was, I don't even know. But it never seemed to stop. Mom and Pop were beyond perplexed as to how they could have raised a child like Caitlyn who they saw as slightly deranged, and we all joked there was a distinct possibility she'd been switched at birth. After a while though, they gave up trying to "fix" her. They just sort of knew no matter the situation, Caitlyn would always believe the opposite of what they did and inevitably find the drama even in a kernel of corn. I personally thought it was kinda neat. She always had something to say that was different and made you think about things from another perspective, even if a good percentage of the time what she had to say wasn't all the way thought through and sounded pretty bonkers. I think for Caitlyn there was no other choice than to question the way things had always been, perhaps 'cause she was a girl of considerable smarts who had big plans for her life but was being raised in a world where women were all supposed to end up like my mom, quiet housewives who made sure food was cooked and there was always fresh coffee in the pot.

Whatever the reason, Caitlyn loomed large as a human tornado around the homestead, on my worst days I couldn't seem to dredge up even a thimbleful of the angst she did. I always followed the rules, completed my chores, went to bed on time, and made decent grades in school. When I turned sixteen and started driving, I was usually home thirty minutes before curfew so I could watch the ten o'clock news with Mom and Pop and talk about what needed accomplished the next day around the farm. Pop would laugh and tell me to go get in some trouble. But despite myself, I never seemed to be able to. The worst I did was skinny-dipping down at the river once in a while with Miles, and have unprotected sex with Mandy simply 'cause we'd get all riled up at inopportune times and couldn't help ourselves. I couldn't even lie properly. When Pop would ask me questions point-blank about this or that, I'd always tell him the truth. Yes, I left the gas tank in the four-wheeler empty. Yep, I forgot to cover the hay bales with a tarp before the rain. Indeed, I *did* ding the side of the milk barn when I was backing up the tractor. Thing is though, as we all got older, we stopped having point-blank discussions about anything at all. There was a sort of weary quiet that settled over Mom, Pop, and me, especially when it came to personal matters. Without ever discussing it, we'd decided we would work out our own problems on our own time in our own way. No need to go nosing into each other's business. Perhaps it was a trust. Perhaps it was a mistake. Perhaps we was all just too exhausted from dealing with Caitlyn's ever maddening frankness. Whatever the case, part of me missed the way Caitlyn would blow things up, make us talk out why we was doing what we was doing, saying what we was saying, and believing what we believed, even if ultimately she could be proved wrong. Sometimes you just go along with things without really questioning if what you're going along with is good for you. And sometimes, going along ain't all it's cracked up to be. I mean, come on now. The world spins. Things change. Nothing will ever be as it once was. That's just the truth of the matter, painful as it might be and much as we might pray it weren't so. You can't just plan on doing things the same way forever. And if you is planning on it, you better sure-as-shit know why. And honestly, I wished I was more like Caitlyn nowadays—able to have the tough conversations, to think outside the box, to give my opinion, to be really truthful about how gigantic the world is and my current, very minuscule place in it. But I ain't my sister. She's all but been run out of here. Lines have been drawn between us and them, even if neither side really knows who is who and what is what. So, fuck!

I clean up the toilet in the bank bathroom after my blowout. It's something I've unfortunately become accustomed to doing these last few months: double/triple flush, wipe off the rim, check the seat, turn on an exhaust fan to air the room out. I wash my hands and my face and look myself in the mirror, and suddenly, I realize I never should have come here looking the way I do, grey-faced, spoilt T-shirt and jeans, baseball cap that's ringed with a sweat stain white as a salt lick. I look like a poor, idiot farmer who don't know his frontside from his backside. I look like I'm the kind of guy who mooches off the system, who can't pay his bills. My sister would've known better than to walk into a place of business looking like a piece of white trash. But then, she weren't no white trash, and I, in fact, was. Still, I had no choice. I was here. I was gonna empty my account to pay what I could of my late mortgage, and then I was gonna go.

The bank is still quiet when I enter the lobby again and look around for Mr. Green. Apparently, he's finished chatting up the cute blonde teller and made his way back to his office. I see him through the blinds on his office window talking on the phone behind his big wooden desk. I suppose I must look slightly confused as to what I want because the blonde teller smiles and waves, "You need Mr. Green?"

"That's right," I say.

"Okay. I'll let him know," she replies, and she picks up a phone receiver. Then, she stops, "What did you say your name was again?"

I'm about to say my name when I hear Mr. Green behind me, "I'll take care of this, Susan."

Mr. Green, whose hair is stark white and thinning, is wearing a watermelon pink dress shirt, grey slacks, the shiniest black patent leather shoes I've ever seen, and a gold watch that sparkles with diamonds around the edges. He waves me back to his office with a closed-lip smile.

As I walk across the carpet, I see him take a seat, once more, behind his desk, and I look around and wonder if everybody in the bank knows why I'm here, that I've missed my last two mortgage payments, and I'm about to pay only half of my third. But none of the other suits seem concerned or even aware of my presence. When I arrive at Mr. Green's office door, he don't get up, just motions to a chair opposite his desk. Clearly, *he* knows why I'm here.

"Have a seat, Calem," he says.

"Thank you," I reply.

"Well, I guess you're in a bit of a pickle, huh?" Mr. Green says breaking the silence.

I nod ashamed, take my baseball cap off reverently and look down at my boots. "Yes, sir."

Mr. Green pecks something into the keyboard of his computer with his index fingers, and I realize he don't know how to type proper, like how my sister used to make fun of me for doing it. He lets out a heavy sigh. "Two months late on your mortgage payments. And I suppose you ain't here to tell me you ain't gonna miss your third."

I look up at him and force a smile. "I'm sure you can see on there somewhere; I have a little money in my savin's account. Not much. But I wondered if we could work out a deal. You know I ain't missed a payment in the last seven years, up until a couple months ago. Thing is, I had a little medical scare that put me back quite a few bucks —"

"Son, your mortgage is less than anybody I ever seen," Mr. Green interrupts, looking at me real harsh.

I can't stand looking back at him, so I stare down at my boots again, and hate myself for wearing 'em in here all dirty on this pretty blue carpet. "Well, I can almost make a full payment with what I got left in my savin's and what I got in my wallet right now," I say.

"You on drugs?" Mr. Green asks.

"What? No, sir," I look up at him, once again.

"I'm tired of folks comin' in here with their sob stories that they got no money 'cause of this or that when really they is just spendin' all their cash on drugs. You said you had a medical scare. You didn't OD?"

Once more, I'm at a loss for words. Then, I shake my head until a somber, "No," manages to escape my mouth. "I decided to come in here 'cause I got the letters y'all sent me, and I wanted you to know what was goin' on, face-to-face, honest and truthful."

"So, what *is* goin' on?" he asks.

I try to swallow, but my mouth is so dry, I end up coughing. "I understand if I miss three payments y'all can start foreclosure proceedings. But I'm here to ask for a little leniency. I'd like to pay as much as I can today—almost a whole payment. Then soon, I'll have the rest of it. I promise. I just...like I said, somethin' unexpected came up, and it's set me back."

"How much you got?" he asks.

"Whatever is in my savin's and this here hundred dollar bill." I grab my wallet out of my back pocket, pull out the Benjamin, and set it on the desk in front of him, knowing even as I do it how ridiculous and insignificant it looks crumpled up there amongst all his printed white papers, glossy pens, and photos of his family that look like the stock pictures that come in frames bought at the store.

Mr. Green pecks the keyboard in front of him again, and squints at his computer monitor, shakes his head with a frustrated sigh. "There are rules, son. There are people I answer to higher up than me that make 'em."

"I'm just askin' for a little understandin', not even for me really, but for my mom and pop. See, they co-signed my mortgage loan, as you may remember, and well, they don't know what's goin' on. And I ain't figured out how to tell 'em just yet. And well, I don't want my problems affectin' them. They got issues of their own. Fact is, I was thinkin' of sellin' the house anyway, or well...they could sell the house even. Just one more month or two, and I know someone would snatch that place right up, and there would be money to pay off everything."

Mr. Green, sighs. "That place sat on the market for two years before you came along, Calem. And the financial climate around here is even worse now. How do you think you're ever gonna sell it in one or two months, let alone one or two years? I'm sorry, but that just ain't realistic. As for your mom and pop, I know all about their issues too. And let's be honest, they can't help you anymore than they can help themselves."

For a moment, I wonder if Mr. Green knows about the co-op situation, or if there's something more I ain't even heard of.

Suddenly, his face softens. He folds his hands and rests them on his desk. "Look, I know things is hard, but they's hard for everybody, and I'm not sure if they's gonna get better here anytime soon." He sighs, looks down at his hands, then back up at me. "My best advice to all y'all is maybe just cut your losses and move on. Life ain't always winnin'. It's sometimes just bad luck. All you can do is face it and try better next time."

"So, you ain't gonna take my money?" I ask, eyeing the hundred dollar bill lying on the desk between us.

"You get in here before the fifteenth with a whole month's mortgage, that will buy you one more month. You pay off all three months, I'll make sure your back payments won't affect your credit one iota. After the fifteenth, though...it's out of my hands, son."

I can't quite figure out if I should thank Mr. Green or tell him to fuck off. I notice him look at the Benjamin on his desk with pity, like he wishes I'd take it off his desk right quick, so I do. I snatch it off his desk and stand. He stands too. There's a look in his eyes of resignation, like I'm just another one of 'em—those poor folks he's probably got lined up down the street who he can't help.

"Thank you for comin' in, Calem. Most people wouldn't even do that." Mr. Green offers his hand to me, and I shake it.

"Thank you too, sir," I say as I turn to go. Then I stop at his doorway and look back. "What you said earlier, everything okay with my mom and pop?" I ask.

Mr. Green gives me another one of those closed-lip banker's smiles of his, one that I know he's got down pat from practicing for years. It's wide and tight and fake as Velveeta cheese. "You best ask them that question, son." And he goes back to pecking at his computer keyboard.

I suppose for him this is just another afternoon. For me, it sure as shit ain't.

I don't remember how I got back to the truck, but suddenly, I'm in it, the engine is running, and I'm waiting at the edge of the highway for a station wagon to drive past before I pull out of the bank parking lot and head in the direction of Mom and Pop's. Everything is blurry in my mind, and all my actions are perfunctory, like I know what I'm doing, but I ain't having to think about any of it. Suddenly, I realize the radio is playing a country song, but it's way too energetic for me, so I flip it off and drive in silence aside from the sound of the wind whipping in the window. It's getting late in the afternoon, and I should roll the window up, but I like the bite of the air on my face, slapping me to remind me to pay attention.

Ahead, the highway widens out where the county blew a hole in a hill to build a bridge across the Big Piney River, and I think I should accelerate towards the bridge, hit the railing with everything I got, and see if it stops me dead on or if I could go flying right through it, off the bridge, and crash into the river below. What a way to die. People would talk about it for years. I suddenly realize I'm accelerating, twenty miles over the speed limit, then twenty-five, then thirty. Then, a minivan appears on the other side of the highway driving towards me, and I let my foot off the gas. This ain't the way I'm doing things, causing problems for everybody else. I ain't breaking a goddamned hole in the bridge. I ain't traumatizing the whole fucking county. I ain't leaving the world with all my troubles. I'm taking 'em with me best I can. I have a plan. I've been formulating it in my head for six months now. I've thought it through like a robber in a bank heist movie. I've figured out everything that could go wrong, and I've taken steps to make sure nothing does.

I grip the steering wheel with sweaty palms and think about how I'll blow my head off with my shotgun in a few hours, after I get home from gigging with Miles, after I've said my good-byes, and made sure everybody knows that me killing myself weren't their fault, and there was nothing they coulda done to stop me. That's real important, that nobody goes around feeling all this blame, especially Miles, 'cause the truth of the matter is, I'm just meeting my maker. Fuck a natural death! Or maybe this *is* natural, these feelings inside of me telling me to leave this world. For all anyone knows a person killing themselves ain't no different than the mass stranding of whales or the sudden death of thousands of fish or birds or insects. Maybe nature knows something we don't, knows how to thin the herd by whispering in certain ears their time on this earth is through. Besides, how is killing yourself really that different than what we do to animals we care for: a dog with cancer, a cow with a broken leg, a horse with a colic? You're putting yourself out of your misery. You're living and dying on your own terms, not anybody else's. The ability of a fully dexterous person to do something about the pain they's feeling, to stop the screaming and the hurt in their head, seems to be very real mercy to me—the surest sign we humans are at the top of the evolutionary pyramid.

Still, you gotta be merciful on the folks you're leaving behind too. You gotta think through what you're doing, how you're gonna do it, when and where, and so on. For me, I know I have to do it before the Night Call begins its reign of terror, but after I've finished all my chores and wrapped up all my loose ends. I'm gonna go in the shower, and over my head, I'm gonna put on one of those thick, waterproof bags you seal up your valuables in when you're floating the river. Maybe the gunshot will blow through the bag, but mostly, I think the mess will be contained.

See, I'm gonna be using a shotgun, which shoots *shot*. That's basically a cartridge made up of hundreds of tiny pellets. Rifles and handguns shoot *loads*, which are cartridges made up of a single bullet. And while pellets of *shot* decimate whatever they hit up close, a *bullet* will go clean through, meaning that while *shot* will obliterate an organ like a brain, shooting a *bullet* in your head has the high probability of leaving you maimed. And that's where people who survive suicide by gun go wrong. You don't fucking shoot yourself with a handgun or a rifle. You find yourself a *shotgun* to do the deed.

I know folks is nervous about guns nowadays, 'cause of some of the things people do with them, 'cause of all the crazies out there. And hey, it's awful when I hear about another goddamned school shooting or that awful incident that happened out in Vegas. I mean, shit! Me, I never looked at a gun as anything but a good time. Still, I get it. There are folks who probably shouldn't have all the power they do behind their trigger finger. Second Amendment or not, guys like Miles scare even me sometimes, especially when he gets drunk and goes off about how he's joined this local militia that's preparing for a civil war they think is brewing just beneath the thin skin of modern America.

We gotta take it back, Miles rails, as though he's sitting pretty behind some cushy anchor desk like Tucker Carlson or Sean Hannity. *We gotta take back America!* It'd almost be laughable if it weren't so sad, if it weren't for the fact my sister is screaming the same damn thing from the other side of the political spectrum. It gets so nuts, sometimes, I wonder if instead of a civil war the far right and far left will end up merging together, like maybe they'll realize they's all pretty much wanting the same damn thing, they've just been screaming so loud and so long over each other, they don't even realize they's two sides of the same radicalized cow patty. I mean, end of the day, everybody just wants freedom to live their fucking lives. Difference is, Miles sees the government as the problem, while Caitlyn thinks the government ain't doing enough. She and all those progressive assholes trot out Blacks and Latinos and gays with all their problems like they is prizes to be won, refusing to acknowledge that *we've* been left behind too, folks like Miles and me and Mom and Pop—*her own people!* Us backwoods types ain't exotic seeming, though. While the heritage of Brown and Black folks is something to be bowed down to, when it comes to us here in the sticks, apparently there ain't no difference if your family origins is German, French, Irish, or fucking Albanian. If you's white, you's trash—slime on the underside of America's shoe, something to be scorned and sloughed off. And sad thing is, we take our lickings, and we make do, and we have for a long, long time. We've been used and abused and fucked over so much, I honestly don't understand how the rest of the country can be shocked that people like them Proud Boys is pissed as hell and talk openly about becoming revolutionaries. Of course, I don't know if any of Miles' comrades are really *that* serious about starting a war. So far as I know none of them was a part of the Capitol riots, though Miles says he wishes he had been. Part of me thinks they just like parading around town in their trucks with their guns like colored gangs drive lowriders and carry heat in the ghetto 'cause it makes 'em feel like they got power. And honestly, I don't think Caitlyn wants to turn us all into carbon-neutral, vegan communists. I think both sides is just frustrated that things ain't better. But like I say, they's coming at the same problem from two different sides. And while they believe with a religious fervor that the other side is the enemy, I figure maybe one day they'll meet in the goddamn middle and realize they was both attempting to fix the same issue the whole time. And the sorry part is, maybe if they'd worked together from the git-go, they coulda figured it all out before so many people had to go through all the hurt and pain that's come with the fighting.

But what do I know? I'm just another fucking hick stuck in the middle of all the political posturing, jostled around like the immigrants and the Blacks and the fucking homos too. Nobody's listening to any of us little guys—not really—or maybe nobody can hear us 'cause of all their damn self-righteous screaming. Some days I wonder if I screamed out loud if somebody would hear *me*? If they did though—if I got their attention for two goddamned seconds—what would I say? What *could* I say? I'm a nobody. I'm a nothing. I don't count in this world.

The sun ain't even set and here it comes already—the Night Call—the thoughts that torment me, so vivid and real, I dream of sucking on the metal end of a shotgun like my mom's teat. I can almost feel the cold steel ping against my teeth, and it makes my mouth water. I can taste the gunpowder tip of my gun, and it's the only thing that soothes me. Soon, my finger will curl around the trigger on my .20 gauge, just like it has since I was twelve years old. I'll hug the barrel like a good friend. It'll be just like I've practiced. But tonight, the relief won't be temporary. Finally, tonight it won't be a dream; it will be real.

And suddenly, I scream out into the wind. I scream out with a lunatic joy I ain't felt in a while. This is my last sunset! This is my last drive down Highway 17! This is the last time I have to think about all that I am not and never will be! Soon, I'll be free!

Filled with an energy I ain't had in a while, I hit the steering wheel and pound the dash and scream again. I turn on the radio hoping some country song I know will be playing. And sure as shit one is! I drive a little faster and sing out with the song like I've never sung anything in my life. It's all about love and loss and drinking and dancing, and I swear to God it's everything I've ever felt but not known how to put into words. For a brief moment, I'm happy. Images of Mandy, Mom and Pop, Miles, the American flag, and hell, even the cows cross my mind, and I'm full of love and gratitude for all of 'em, for the setting sun, and the wind in my face, for all the life I've ever had! Sure, there's part of me that wishes I could hold on to those things I love. But I can't. Even the guy singing the song blasting in my ears knows you can't. Nobody can hold on, not forever. And that's the secret, ain't it? You can't hold on, not now, not ever. So, why are we trying so damn hard? You're born on a cliff's edge and most of us spend our lives trying not to fall off, attempting to cling to existence with a single goddamn finger. It's exhausting and impossible. One day, you're gonna have to let go and fall into whatever comes next. Me, I'm taking that fall with a smile on my face. I'm letting go with both hands, thank you very much!

It almost arouses me, this sudden feeling of lightness. I touch my crotch and feel a spark shoot up through my body, something I ain't felt in forever. I think about that girl at Kell's and Mandy and Miles' ex-wife and her girlfriend Fantasia. My pants tighten, and I reach down to adjust my cock so it can grow upwards in my jeans. Fuck! Where the hell did this come from? Suddenly, the ecstasy I was feeling before becomes something more, something wondrous, like the hello of a lost friend, the touch of an old lover, the angelic chorus of heaven! I laugh at myself. I'm so hungry, I'm delirious. I'm so tired and worn-out, I'm punch-fucking-drunk. I'm so wasted away, I'm already half-gone. I ain't thinking, and that's why I'm suddenly hard as a rock. I'm like I used to be back before I was threatened with accusations of rape, back when I thought there was maybe something like hope out there for people like me, back when I had the distraction of imagining a wife and kids and a future. Fuck, I miss those times. I miss that sense of...well, possibility.

And suddenly, all the happiness and joy rushing over me fades like the sun going down in the distance. And I can't even remember what euphoria feels like or why I was smiling or singing or screaming. I'm cold now and starving. The wind is biting a little too hard. I roll up the window and turn off the radio. And I remember the one last thing I gotta do. I gotta call Caitlyn, and say my goodbye to *her*.

I dig for my cell phone and hold it in my hand. This is the one thing I don't want to do. She won't be there, of course. She never is. I'll have to leave her a message. And maybe that's why I've been scared to call 'cause I'll have to leave a voicemail, and she'll play it over and over, trying to decode the words, struggling to translate the tone of my voice into some explanation about why I took my life. But I can't explain to her why I'm going to do what I'm going to do. I can barely explain it to myself. I just know what I have to do. So, my plan is to tell her I was thinking about her and the kids and Dan, and that the weather is making everything real pretty down here with the changing colors of the trees—even if that ain't true. Then, I'll tell her I love her, I think she's pretty great, and I'm proud of all she's done with her life. And the truth is, I am.

I've practiced my message to Caitlyn over and over in my head the last few weeks. I know it like lines in a movie. Still, it's harder than I imagined to actually call now that I have to. But I got no choice. It's only gonna get harder from here. I have to suck it up, and finally, I do it. I punch her name in my cell and lift the phone to my ear. It rings and rings and rings. Then, just as I expect to hear her voicemail greeting telling me to leave a message, I hear a click, and on the other end of the line, Caitlyn says, "Hey, little brother."

G rowing up, Caitlyn and me didn't squabble like most kids. Maybe this was because we were so far apart in age it seemed a bit unfair for her—the older sister—to treat me poorly, or for me—the kid brother—to annoy a person I saw as practically an adult. Sure, I didn't understand much of the highfalutin things she went on about most of my growing up years, but I did find it all interesting, even if mostly it made me chuckle. And just the same, she would laugh at me for the things I talked about too, but her giggling was usually in good humor 'cause, she assured me, she found me equal parts fascinating and confounding as well. That's not to say we never fought. I'm sure we had little spats here and there over dumb stuff like me accidentally breaking a bottle of her perfume or her unknowingly throwing out a jar of catfish bait she thought was spoilt strawberries. Whatever our quarrels, they was mostly so insignificant as to make them quickly forgettable, and we did.

Truth is, we both genuinely liked each other 'cause no matter if she despised me going out and hunting, and I chaffed at her being so particular and perfect, we was in the same boat—two kids growing up out in the middle of the country without much going for us other than that. Even after she left home, married Dan and had kids, me and Caitlyn was good siblings to each other. We would catch up every few weeks on the phone about our vastly differing lives. These was enjoyable talks too, not stifled or forced. Mostly, I think we was just honest, and that reality we shared with one another made us both laugh at how unique the world could be depending on where you lived and the space you took up in it. I knew Caitlyn saw me as a hick, and I didn't try to deny it. In fact, I knew she enjoyed being regaled with the latest gossip of my provincial, backwoods life, whether those stories was about local crime, torrid redneck affairs, or county politics. And I knew Caitlyn was only ever becoming more and more citified, but I, too, found her stories about suburban sprawl, municipal theatrics, and politically correct housewife spectacles just as wondrous. Back then, tiny disparities in our lives were no real threat to either of us. And I imagine our shared world views coulda complemented each other forever if not for that thing that happened, that thing that shook the world, that impossible reality that became real, the election of Donald Trump as commander in chief of the United States of America.

Like so many people, I remember where I was when I heard the news. I had just finished cleaning the barn after milking and made my way up to the house for a cup of fresh coffee. Mom was in front of the stove like always, and when she handed off the cup of joe I was after, she said—like it was some slightly surprising but not altogether awful news—Donald Trump had won the election. Yes, I had voted for him, just like everybody else I knew, but I guess I was slightly surprised as well. I mean, it seemed that Clinton was bound to win the whole kit and caboodle in a landslide. And I guess she did, in a way. She got the popular vote, but of course, we all found out that don't really matter much, not with the way our so-called democracy works.

Anyway, while I wasn't exactly over the moon about Trump, I knew Caitlyn would be devastated. We'd had talks about it. She begged me not to vote for him and pleaded with me to make sure Mom and Pop didn't either. She told me if we did, we'd regret it 'cause, well, he was just so damn awful. Truth was, I didn't like the way he made fun of people or some of the things he said. I mean, hell, he definitely had a morally questionable point of view that bothered most folks, even those of us who weren't all that religious. But that damn Clinton seemed squirrelly to me too. So, what difference did it make really? If there was any reason I would've voted for Clinton, it was for my sister 'cause I know how happy having a woman president would've made her. In the end, though, all Clinton talked was pie-in-the-sky bullshit that sounded good but seemed a little unrealistic. And, well, honestly, I liked how Trump talked about us rural folk—the backbone of America—and how *we* was what was important. He seemed to believe in us, and he made us feel energetic about our lives in a way no one had in a while.

I called Caitlyn that afternoon knowing I'd get an earful regarding the election results. And when I got her voicemail, I didn't think nothing of it. I left a message. I told her to call me back. And I imagined she would in a couple hours after she'd put the kids down for their nap or later that night after they'd all had dinner. But she didn't call back that evening. She didn't call back the next day neither, nor the day after that. I asked my mom if she'd talked to Caitlyn, but she'd left Caitlyn a couple voicemails as well, and she hadn't heard a peep. One week on, Mom finally called Dan who told her Caitlyn was having a hard time over the election, and she would ring us back when she was feeling better. This behavior upset Mom partly because she thought it was silly, but really because I think my mom felt slightly guilty, just like I did. The election was similar to so many other times in our lives when Caitlyn had appealed to us to see things her way, and well, we just couldn't. But I think this time what we'd done had really broke her, made her feel like she didn't matter and all the stuff she cared about didn't matter. And if she didn't matter to us, she wasn't going to let us matter to her, not no more.

It was almost a year before Mom and Caitlyn finally spoke on the phone. Mom wanted to see the grandkids, but Caitlyn just wasn't having it. With Mom's encouragement, I sent Caitlyn a few texts, which she responded to, but everything was changed. Eventually, I got Caitlyn on the line myself, but the differences in our worlds was no longer a delight. Everything had suddenly become so serious. And while I still liked the way it seemed Trump was looking out for rural America—cutting regulations, lowering taxes, signing trade deals with Canada that could help our dairy industry by opening up our ability to export—I also understood he was a shady character who embarrassed the United States just as often as he gave us reason to be proud. And I realized you can't go around saying all politicians is corrupt, that they's all the same, and who you vote for don't matter, but then go put politics before family, before morals, before decency, before everything that's honestly important. Fact is, Clinton probably woulda been just about the same as Trump. No, that ain't true. She woulda been better. She woulda been nicer, more decent, more like how people want the world to be. Caitlyn was right.

"Hey, sis," I say, adjusting a little uncomfortably in the cab of my truck. "I didn't expect you to pick up."

"Well, why'd you call then?" Caitlyn asks, half-joking.

"I was gonna leave you a message," I say, and I roll the window up a little tighter to make sure I can hear alright.

"Sorry. You want me to hang up, and you can call back?"

I smile. "No. No, not at all."

"Whatcha doing?" she asks.

"Headin' home to do the evenin' milkin'. I was out runnin' errands."

"Sounds like fun. Dan took the boys for a happy meal. They were absolute terrors this afternoon. I told him he was gonna be a widow if he didn't do something quick. I'm picking up toys all over the house as we speak." I can hear the frustration in Caitlyn's voice, but I can also hear her amusement at her own predicament.

Searching for something to say, I offer, "Wade's cafe closed down."

"Finally."

"What do you mean, finally?"

"Calem, that place was a grease pit. The only thing they served there was fat with a side of salt."

"That's rich coming from the woman who just sent her kids to McDonald's for dinner," I shoot back.

On the other end of the line, I imagine Caitlyn rolling her eyes, "They only eat off the healthy menu, and they get the apple slices, not fries. Besides, it's not every day."

I laugh, "I also thought you didn't support Mickey D's 'cause they don't pay their employees a livin' wage or somethin' like that. At least Wade's was a local business with local roots."

"You know what, sorry I said anything," Caitlyn says, and I hear her pop the can on a soda or perhaps it's one of her fancy favored waters. "But wait 'til you have kids, little brother, then you'll understand."

For a moment, the way Caitlyn has imagined so thoroughly that I will have kids breaks my heart, and I quickly change the subject. "Hatcher Mings' folks overdosed last night."

"What? That's awful."

"Yeah. Looks like Shelly is gonna make it, but they ain't sure about Rhett."

"What did they overdose on?"

"Some sort of fentanyl-laced somethin', I 'spect. Though, Mom said it might've been prescription."

"Drug companies. They only care about the almighty dollar. Don't matter who suffers."

"People is in pain," I say. Then I bite my lip, wish I hadn't said nothing about people hurting. I don't want to hear Caitlyn launch into one of her liberal tirades about how us rural folks have brought it on ourselves with our blind dedication to guns and God and lower taxes.

"You don't have to tell me that," she says. "I've been volunteering at the women's shelter up here. Those girls have been through things you wouldn't believe. Half of 'em are only there because they lost their jobs and have no other place to live. Some of 'em have kids. Most of 'em are alcoholics or drug addicts. Some have been kicked out by their families because they're lesbian. And some of them are sixty-year-old women who've shown up with their faces split open by husbands who've been abusing 'em for years. Talk about pain. They're usually in such a bad place by the time they arrive on our doorstep, I'm surprised they're even able to walk in at all."

I say nothing. I think about my own terrible state and feel ashamed for thinking I'm anything like these women Caitlyn is talking about, but

I am. I can walk, but inside I crawl. I can speak, but the voice that comes out of me ain't my own. It belongs to a skeleton rotting away in a dungeon.

"What do you do to help 'em?" I ask.

"Well, you know, we give 'em food and a safe place to rest their head. If they need physical or emotional treatment, we offer that too. I've been helping a couple girls learn how to balance their checkbooks and apply for food stamps so they can buy groceries for their kids."

"What do you do if they…" I know I shouldn't finish my question, so I don't. And I hope Caitlyn will leave my half-asked question alone, but of course, she doesn't.

"What?" she pries.

"I mean, if they want to die, what do you do then?"

"Well, you know, if they're suicidal, usually they don't come looking for help from us. No, those types, they just…well, you know, they kill themselves."

"That happen a lot?"

"I don't really know. That's just so far afield of our purview."

"A women's shelter," I say, and I wonder if there's a place like that for men.

Almost as though reading my mind, Caitlyn says, "Yeah, just women. No men. They don't really have places for men. I suppose that's 'cause men are too stubborn to ask for help. Lord knows." And she laughs a little laugh, which I know comes from a good place.

"But otherwise, everything is good for you and Dan and the kids?" I ask, wanting to lighten the mood.

"Oh, you know. Taylor is struggling in school, and he's obsessed with hotrods and girls. I'm horrified that I've raised a son whose first thought in the morning is about NASCAR. And Robbie, well, thankfully, he's a lot more like me. He doesn't know the meaning of any grade aside from an A or an A+. He came home crying the other day, and I thought something terrible had happened. He said his teacher had given his best friend, Tippy, a B for a writing assignment, and he couldn't understand for the life of him why. To be honest, it was kind of funny. He's so sweet and gentle. I wonder if he's gay or transgender maybe. Dan and I have talked about it, and we try to make sure the boys know we're open-minded, but well, there's only so much you can do."

"And Dan? How's his job goin'?" I ask.

"Well, he's been driving up to Kansas City more often than either of us would like. They're opening an office there, and he's helping with all the training. Good thing is, they gave him a raise. Money always softens hardship. If anyone knows that firsthand it's you and me, and well, Mom and Pop."

I let out a little laugh that I know Caitlyn wants to hear, like I agree with her or understand or I don't know...relate. Suddenly, all I want to do is get off the phone. I feel so anxious, my stomach kicks me hard, and I try to figure out a way to wrap things up. "Well, that's good to hear. Congratulations," I offer.

Caitlyn sighs. "Yeah, well. How are you doing?" she asks almost like it's some sort of obligatory annoyance.

I think about all the ways I could answer her question, but replying honestly is impossible. So, I say, "I'm alright. Delivered some walnuts over to Kell's earlier. Stopped by the bank. Goin' giggin' with Miles tonight."

"Oh, man, fried hogsuckers on the riverbank sounds amazing."

"Yeah, I'm lookin' forward to it." Suddenly, I remember I forgot to grab a propane tank for the cooker. "You know what, I just realized, I need to call Mom and see if she has a propane tank I can use for tonight. Otherwise, I gotta go back into town and pick one up." I slow down my truck and pull off the road onto a little turnout.

"Oh, gosh," Caitlyn says, "Well I'm sure they'll have one, what with the way Mom likes her grill."

"You should call them too, you know," I tell Caitlyn.

There's a slight hesitation and an inaudible sigh from Caitlyn. "I will. We just get busy, and I forget."

"No, really." I know my voice sounds serious, and suddenly, the truck is way too quiet, sitting there on the side of the road like it is. "You should call them," I reiterate.

"Everything okay?" she asks.

Now it's my turn to hesitate before answering. "They's havin' trouble with the co-op."

"What do you mean?"

"I mean, the co-op is wantin' to kick our dairy to the curb. It's too expensive for them to come all the way out to our place for a drop or two of milk."

"Well, that's crazy. Pop practically started that co-op."

"I know, but that's what we heard."

"*What you heard?* You made it sound so certain."

"It is."

"Not if it's gossip."

I want to argue with her. I mean, *come on!* With the way things have gone around this place, does she really think something as awful as us losing our business, our damn lifeblood, our only hope, is out of the question? Instead, I don't say a thing, and I can tell it annoys her that I'm not arguing with her, like by saying nothing I'm disagreeing just as loudly.

She sighs. "Look, I'll give them a call. Pop shoulda switched over to that organic co-op they started in Paul's Bluff a few years back. Dan and I both told him to."

"With what money? It takes three years at least to turn your dairy into a USDA organic complyin' operation."

"He always seems to have the money to buy land," Caitlyn states matter-of-factly.

This I couldn't argue with, but land meant more to Pop than money. Land was air for him. It was security. Talk about lifeblood. I finally say, "I gotta go."

"Dammit, Calem. Don't be pissy with me. You got nothing to be pissy about. You all live out there in the middle of nowhere. The only people you've got to answer to are yourselves. I mean, it's paradise, right? Come live in the city with all the noise and the traffic and the schedule of things to do, and then you can complain."

I close my eyes and hold back whatever emotion is roiling inside of me. I ain't sure if it's anger or sadness or fucking happiness that soon I won't have to deal with none of this anymore—this upside-down world.

"Yeah well, I'm sure you're right," I say quietly.

"I am. I always am. Well, mostly I am," she laughs, trying to make light of what has become another tense moment to file away with all the rest of them between us these days.

I don't laugh back. Not this time. This time I listen for her breath and imagine the way she was when we were little, playing "old times" up in the run-down church, her bossing me and the cats around, pretending with an imagination that could make me believe we were indeed living in the 1800s, and I needed to go shoot a deer or head off to fight the Civil War. I tell myself to hang on to the sound of her voice. Listen to the ripple of the crick of her soul. It's there beneath all the bullshit.

"Calem?" she asks.

"Yup," I answer, eyes clenched.

"I love you, little brother. You know that, right?"

"Yup. I love you too," I respond.

Silence.

And suddenly, I wish she'd ask me if I was alright, if I was hanging in there. If she asked me right now in this moment, I would tell her everything. I'd bare my fucking soul to her. I'd beg her—*beg her*—to come home. I remember her kissing my knee one time when we was little. I had tripped and fallen and swore my knee was broken. In an instant, she made everything alright. Maybe she could do that again, even if this time it wasn't simple as a hurt knee.

But instead, on the other end of the line, I hear her sigh. "You enjoy one of those hogsuckers for me."

"I will," I say.

"And don't forget to find some propane."

"I won't."

"Alright. We'll talk to you later then," she says.

For a moment, I hang on to her last syllables and consonants and wish with all my heart they won't evaporate from my ears, but they do. So, I say, "Talk to ya later."

And the line goes dead.

I sit in my truck. I don't know how long I sit there. I just do, seeing nothing, hearing nothing, feeling nothing. I remember somebody saying one time, all your brain does is dream. Even when you's awake, it's all still a dream. If it starts to rain, your brain dreams what will happen if you stand under that rain, and then, it will imagine where you need to go and what you need to do to avoid getting wet. And once you're safe from the rain, it will dream what needs to happen next. If you're hungry, your brain will tell you what you want to eat, and if you're hungry enough, it will dream a way to guide you there. If you need to shit, it will imagine what happens if you don't make it to a toilet soon. On and on it goes, dream after dream after dream, thought after thought after thought, nothing but hallucinations ushering us from one moment to the next, leading our bodies through existence. We get suckered into believing that we're our own masters, but really, the "conscious" world is as batshit crazy as the "subconscious" one, and we're just along for the ride—a bag of flesh and bones controlled by a three-pound organ that has its own agenda: eat, sleep, procreate, repeat.

The movies show us stories of zombies taking over the world, out for blood, eaters of flesh, unaware of their own existence. Well, what the movies don't tell you is we're all zombies already. Who needs blood and gore to prove you've been possessed? Take a look at a single mom on food stamps trying to feed four kids while holding down a shit job. Take a look at a teenager around here who don't know what the future holds for him after the lackluster education he got at our local high school. Take a look at a goddamned farmer or a grocery store clerk or a gas station attendant. They're all fucking zombies, man. Suckers indeed. They're puppets of their brains, hanging on for I don't know what reason other than to do what their brains tell 'em. You can be down for the count. You can be dying of fucking cancer, pain leaching through every bone in your body, and still, your brain will tell you that you want to live. It will dream of something better. It will give you hope. And you'll believe it. Even as you're lying there dying, your brain will be the last thing to go 'cause it's not just an organ, it's an *organism* that tells your body you're alive when the truth is it's ALL JUST A FUCKING DREAM!

Suddenly, a car goes flying by outside, and I come to, so to speak. I realize I gotta get going or I'll be late for bringing up the cows for their evening milking, and I know how that will make Pop pissy and how him being pissy will make me feel. I can see it—that dream or thought or whatever you want to call it—vividly like it was real, right in front of me. And suddenly, my brain is imagining what I need to do to make my way back to the farm to avoid making Pop pissy and making me feel like shit. Press the brake. Throw the truck into gear. Look out both side-view mirrors to check for traffic. Tap the gas pedal. Slowly, the truck lurches forward. I hear the tires crunch gravel, then hit the highway, and I accelerate a little more. No sooner am I flying along the highway, than I remember, once again, that I need propane, but I'll just have to cross my fingers Mom has a tank I can borrow. She'll be slightly irritated with me for asking, but she'll have one, I'm almost positive. I think I could call her, but there's no point. I don't have time to go back into town now anyway.

When I get to Mom and Pop's, I go up to the house and root around for some left-overs in the fridge. I find green bean casserole and fried chicken. I don't even throw 'em in the microwave or put 'em on a plate. I eat 'em straight out of the fridge cold, their greases making 'em all firm and jellied. I know Pop is already down at the barn, but I wonder where Mom is? She usually never misses an opportunity to scold me for eating out of one of her Tupperware dishes like I'm some sort of animal. Not that her nagging has ever stopped me. Why dirty an extra plate or bowl? I could lick the plastic container clean, I'm so hungry, but I don't. I put it in the dishwasher and wipe the oil off my hands before grabbing a mug to fill with hot coffee. Mom always makes a fresh pot right before milking time, and today is no exception.

I stand there in the kitchen looking out the window at Mom's garden, which is pretty much done for the year, and that swing set she and Pop bought for the grandkids, which they've hardly ever used. I wish for a moment I could transport myself back twenty years, ten even. I imagine what I might do differently if I knew back then what I do now. I see myself fifteen years old, sitting at the kitchen counter all muscle and spunk, eating everything I can get my hands on and drinking a half-gallon of milk at one meal alone. Back then, I only ever wanted to be outside in nature from the moment I woke up 'til the time I went to bed. I didn't care what I was doing long as I got to be outside. And milking cows seemed like about the best career a guy could have. Fervently, I believed my parents had the greatest life two people could ask for, and I was determined to wind up just like them, probably even with two kids: one boy and one girl. Of course, when you're a child you can't see the realities of life like you can when you get older. Maybe it's 'cause your brain ain't developed enough to look for 'em. Or perhaps, you *can't* see 'em 'cause everything is so new. When things is new, you don't see them like you do after you get used to 'em. It's only later you can see the nuance that was always there—the detail. Like how when you're young a tree is just a tree or a flower is just a flower. But after you get older, you can identify the difference between a birch leaf and a sycamore leaf or a daisy and a coneflower. Then, you get even older, and you can decipher even more, like if a tree is healthy and if a flower is fresh or is about to wither and die.

I decide I better head down to the milk barn. So, I slip on my boots and step outside where the sky is turning pink and red, blushing hard after a romantic golden orb of sun now slinking along the tree line. As I look out over the yard towards the fields and forests, I see things the way I did as a kid, a perfect slice of heaven stretching on forever around me. Then, I refocus my gaze and the picture becomes less pristine. The adult in me is suddenly aware of the tatters of what used to be a thriving farm. I see rust where gleaming metal used to shine. I see rot where once stood proud timbers. Forget the co-op, forget the government, forget the bank. Anybody could tell if they *really looked,* this place ain't no paradise—not no more. It's a diseased patient on its last legs, gasping for breath, already done in, whether it knows it or not. I thought we was friends this place and me. I thought I was taming it, that I was its master. But I've realized we ain't nothing more than servants to this natural world, me and Mom and Pop. We's beggars out here in these woods, tatters of humanity enshrouded in flora and fauna that nibbles away at us day after day, hour by hour, centimeter by centimeter. Weeds and insects and bacteria reign supreme over our stupid, little, temporary accomplishments. Eat. Sleep. Procreate. Repeat.

I hear raised voices in the barn before I reach to open the door, and I know Mom and Pop are having a quarrel, something I ain't heard 'em do in years. Unfortunately, because of the echo inside the milking stage, I can't make out what they's saying, and I creep closer to the door, not sure if I should eavesdrop, announce my presence, or take me a little walk. Surely, they heard me pull up in my truck earlier. Surely, they know I'm around. Before I can decide what I should do, Holly rounds the corner and begins barking at me poised there next to the door like I'm some sort of intruder. Dumb dog. Instantly the voices inside go silent, and next thing I know, Mom is opening the door to the barn, looking at me with red eyes and a sallow face.

"Oh, good. You got some coffee," she says, eyeing the coffee mug in my hand.

"Yeah," I answer quietly. I want to reach out and touch her, to make sure she's okay, but I don't. Pop is standing there watching, hands on his hips, clearly upset. Also, Mom don't like to be fussed over.

"Rhett Mings came out of his coma," Mom offers, to break the silence.

"That's great," I say.

"Still too early to tell if there's brain damage, but looks like he'll survive anyway."

"I'm sure Hatcher is relieved."

"You get something to eat?" Mom asks.

"Yeah, I rooted around in your left-overs up in the fridge."

Finally, Pop pipes in, "We milking here, or are you two gonna just keep prattlin' on?"

Mom raises her hand to stop Pop from saying more. "I'm gettin' out of your hair. Don't you worry none." And Mom moves past me for the house.

Just then, I remember. "Mom, you have a little propane left on your grill I can borrow for tonight?"

She turns back to me. "Sure, sweetie. You just come get it when you're done milkin'."

The way she says "sweetie," the way she's so agreeable, makes me feel worried instead of comforted. "Thank you," I say. "Really appreciate it."

Mom smiles and turns back for the house, and I turn back to Pop who I find looking at me the same way Mom just did, like a doctor about to tell a patient he's gonna die.

"What's goin' on?" I ask.

Pop don't answer. Instead, he exits the milking stage, heads for the back of the barn where the four-wheelers sit. Suddenly, I feel panicked. This wasn't the way I wanted things to go, not on our last night of milking together. I quickly chase after Pop before he can start up his four-wheeler and pretend he don't hear me over the thunder of the engine.

"Pop!" I say.

Pop spins on his heels and furrows his brows at me like I'm some sorta mangy dog that's got in his way. "What?"

"What's goin' on?"

"We's milkin'."

I huff unable to hide my frustration and not wanting to neither. "I'm talkin' about with you and Mom."

"That ain't none of your business," Pop spits.

"Well, it is my business 'cause—" Suddenly, I'm at a loss for words. Instead of trying to find 'em again, I push forward. "Just tell me why you guys was all blown up at each other like two farm cats."

Pop sighs, leans on one hip and looks out at the evening sky before looking back at me resigned. "What do you think it was about? It was about what Delmar Munson said earlier."

"Pop, he don't know everything. You can't be sure what he said wasn't just idle gossip."

"It weren't no gossip," Pop says. "I called up Evelyn over in Bill's office. She confided in me that it was all true. They's fixin' to vote us out of the co-op."

I want to argue, if anything to make Pop feel better about the whole situation, but there ain't no point. "You get a sense of when they's gonna do it?" I ask.

"No idea," Pop says as he swats his pant leg with the gloves in his hand sending off a little dirt cloud out into the air. "Wish they'd wait until the new year, but you know how folks is. They get an idea in their head—especially if it makes 'em uncomfortable—they want it over and done with soon as possible so they can move on with their lives."

"Pop, I'm sorry."

"Yeah, well. It ain't your fault," he shrugs. "Like I said earlier, I need to sell this whole lot and you should go find yourself a decent job."

There was a tremble in Pop's voice, a terror I ain't ever heard in my entire life, and I wonder if I should make up an excuse to go get something out of my truck so if he's gonna shed a tear, I won't see it.

Before I can move a muscle, he continues on, "I guess what sours me more than sellin' the cows and the barn and all the equipment is that I'm gonna have to sell Cantrell's and probably some of our own farm to make do until my retirement comes on."

"Yeah, well. Those kids is always bustin' through that fence to get to that damn waterfall," I offer like it's some sort of consolation. "It's been more annoyin' than just about anything to be out there every few months cleanin' up all that shit they leave. Ain't a lot of good huntin' on Cantrell's either," I say, but I'm lying. The hunting on Cantrell's is great, and Pop knows it.

"Some yahoo is gonna move in there, clear cut all them old trees, and use 'em for firewood, probably block our view with some monster house," Pop says.

"Come on now. Who's gonna do that? Ain't nobody movin' to these parts. If anything, folks is tryin' to get gone."

Pop doesn't say nothing, kicks a clod of manure with the toe of his boot. Then, he looks off at the twilight sky falling over the fields. "Your Mom is mad at me 'cause of how all this is gonna affect you. She says she told me I shoulda discouraged you from bein' a dairy farmer like me way back when. She says I knew things was only gonna get worse, and there was no way you could hold on to this little operation of ours no matter if you got every single thing plumb near perfect."

"Pop, I wanted to be a farmer. You couldn't have discouraged me otherwise," I say.

"Yeah, I could've. I coulda directed you different. I sure as hell didn't *dis*-courage you," he says. "Trust me when I tell you, I've been thinkin' about our situation all day. I've been thinkin' about it for two or three years now, wishin' somehow somethin' would change, would break in our favor. I've come at this problem we got here from every which way you can imagine. Thing is, I don't know what I coulda done different except not get you involved, which your mom is right about."

"Stop sayin' that. You act like I didn't have a choice in the matter, but I did. I *do*! Just like Caitlyn chose to leave, I chose to stay. I made that choice. Me. Not you. Not Mom. Me."

Pop shakes his head. He doesn't want to argue. Instead of looking back at me, this time he just keeps staring out at that sky turning dark. "Poor Rhett Mings. I can't help wonderin' if he and Shelly wanted to die, to get away from this place. And now they brought him back from the edge of Lord knows where to return to this hell hole and probably without all his facilities too."

I can't tell if Pop despises the Mings for almost killing themselves or thinks they almost got it right. I wish I could ask, but it terrifies me to know what he'd say, to know how he'll judge me when I take my leave of this world. Instead, I figure I ought to change the subject. No need to go wallowing any longer in self-pity—not tonight. No, this evening I'm determined to make sure Pop knows none of this is his fault; it's just fucking luck of the draw. I swallow back all my emotion, stick out my chest a little, and force a smile onto my face. "Pop," I say.

He don't turn back to me. "Yeah," he answers.

"Let's go get the cows. It's past their milkin' time already, and there's enough sufferin' around this place without involvin' them in it too. Poor things. Their teats is probably draggin' the ground."

After a beat, Pop says, "Yup."

But Pop don't move, so I try to lighten the mood again. "I ever tell you, I got 'em all named?" I ask.

"Who?"

"Them cows."

Even from behind I can see Pop grin. "You and me both then, I guess," Pop says, and he turns to me. His eyes are wet, but he ain't shed a tear. Not him. "I'm sure the names I've come up with are better than yours, though," he winks at me.

"I got a few four-letter ones that might surprise you."

Pop lets out a chuckle. Then, he takes a breath and slaps his gloves against his jeans again. "Well, we better go get 'em."

He heads for his four-wheeler, his body limping and ragged from years a tough work, full of more hard angles than soft spots, and I wish I could ask him if he sees the world even worse than I do, if he realizes it's all so pointless? Does he know we's just organisms? Does he understand we's just here to eat, sleep, procreate, and repeat? And if he does—if he gets it—how does he put up with it? How does he push on? But Pop don't look back at me. No, he just starts up his four-wheeler and drives off down towards the cow pasture. And I think, I gotta hurry up, or he'll be mad at me for dawdling back behind. Then, for a brief moment,

I wonder where missing somebody factors into this existence of ours? Whatever evolutionary use it may or may not have, I'm gonna miss that old man when I'm gone. I'm gonna miss him more than he'll ever know.

'spect some folks could never off themselves 'cause they're worried about what comes after. Not me. What do you call those tendrils of light that shimmer across a surface when the sun reflects off the water? It's like the opposite of a shadow, that twinkling glow. It's gotta have a name, something more than just reflection, some word to match the beauty of its hypnotic dance. It only lasts for a little while, until the sunshine goes away. Whatever it's called, that light-I-don't-know-the-name-of is one of the most dazzling displays the heavens give us. It finds even the darkest nook or cranny and turns it into something magical if only for a little while. I have lain on the pebble carpet of a riverbank, under the blazing sun, and watched as that dancing light moves from the underside of green tree leaves to lichen-laced boulders to mudbanks and sand. For as long as the day allows, I have been stupefied by those glimmers, lulled into a calm I have otherwise never known on this earth. And while I don't have much confidence in heaven or hell, I do believe that whatever comes after the blood stops pumping through a person's veins is akin to that wordless light—alive yet inanimate, fixed yet kinetic, ephemeral yet permanent, everywhere yet nowhere.

I suppose I sound like a loon talking about such foolishness. Most folks around here would be scandalized if they knew the notions leaping to the front of my noggin about how religion ain't nothing but a Band-Aid to shield the weaker of us from the fact we's just another form of existence worth nothing more than the impression we make when we're alive and the echo we leave behind us when we die. There's something about being out in nature, surrounded by all the life and death that churns in one square inch of soil, that makes a person question the simplemindedness of faith compared to the boundless possibility of fact.

When you realize something as seemingly insignificant as a worm or a butterfly or a bacteria have infinite sizes and shapes and colors and responsibilities on this planet with wildly differing means of eating and shitting and breeding and dying, you can't help but know beyond a shadow of a doubt we don't grasp a razor's edge of the great unknown that we think we do, and anyone who says different is a fool or a liar.

One time, I tried to share these thoughts of mine about the hereafter with Miles. I wondered if perhaps he might feel the same. He said he didn't want to talk about what comes after or what came before this here life. He likes believing in something that allows him the hope maybe he'll see his mom and pop again someday. Caitlyn, too, goes to church and believes in the whole kit-and-caboodle, though, I'm pretty sure if she really thought about it, she only frequents the spiritual like some people smoke—socially. I suppose that's the one commonality between the left and the right, whether they'd admit it or not—they all like to trust in some higher power, some voodoo grand scheme being played out by forces unseen. And I guess that's where I differ from the rest of the world. I'm simply not convinced as to the verity of such nonsense. Sure, I like church. I go every Sunday, and Lord knows I've whispered out a prayer a time or two, but dammit-all if I don't reckon the only thing I have is here and now, and when my time on this earth is through, I won't have to worry about nothing more. There's a relief in that. No almighty God or Satan or heaven or hell. Just done and done.

Perhaps, I feel this way 'cause back when I was thirteen, I saw someone die right in front of my eyes. My folks had taken Caitlyn and me down to the Current River to go floating. They rented us all inner tubes from a little tour company who put us in about five miles north of their operation and assured us if we only stopped to have lunch for thirty or forty minutes on a gravel bar somewhere, we should be down exactly to where they planned to pick us up at four that afternoon.

For some reason, no one else was on the river that day, and I'm not sure why. It was damn near 'bout perfect weather, crystal clear water, cloudless skies, and just enough of a breeze to chill your skin and keep you cool from the sizzle of the sun. I remember how when we all got into the water that morning, there was laughter and excitement at the possibility of adventure that lay ahead of us. Even Caitlyn, who could sometimes scowl at the thought of anything naturalistic, was unusually cheerful, her hair pulled back in a knot and no make-up on her face to speak of. Pop was the one who had got it in his craw we should all go floating, but Mom was the one who'd figured out all the details. She'd called ahead and sussed out the best place to rent inner tubes. Then, she'd thrown lunch together in a couple waterproof bags we could float behind us. And most importantly, she'd made sure Pop remained optimistic about the venture as the day to go grew near. For Pop, it was hard to leave the herd and the milking to hired hands, and it wasn't just about the fact when he did so it cost him most of his profit for that day, but he was like me, he enjoyed his time in the milk barn. And I genuinely believe, like me, he missed it. Still, at that particular moment in time, things was good for our dairy. And if you could get Pop out of his head about his worries, you could have a pretty darn good time with him.

Thirty minutes after we'd settled into our rubber rafts and scared the bejesus out of the fish and crawdads and everything else with our whooping and hollering, a calm settled over our little group. And aside from the occasional hand or foot that slipped almost silently in and out of the water as a make-shift inner tube rudder, all you could hear was the gentle lap of the current moving you along, the rustle of the tree canopy overhead, and the occasional plop of a turtle or frog into the water. Somehow, I'd ended up in the back of the pack, and it was a nice view, watching Mom and Pop and Caitlyn all content, their pale, country bodies cast gold in the warm glow of sunbeams. It was one of those rare times when I don't believe a one of us was thinking about the tenterhooks on which we existed, our cares having evaporated from our minds like dewdrops under the morning light. And just when I thought the moment couldn't have been more perfect, we rounded a bend to find a doe and her fawn, legs tall as stilts, necks stretched out like giraffes, black noses nuzzling the water just beneath a small clearing. They didn't hear us approaching, and no one in my family realized they was there either until we was all spitting distance of one another. Then suddenly, like magic, we all locked eyes. Our necks craned just slightly, but there was no fear or panic or undue excitement from either party, just an understanding of two families meeting in the wild on a beautiful day.

Once we was on down the river and out of earshot of the deers, Pop spun himself around, grinning wide as a cat. "Y'all see that?"

Everyone answered in the affirmative.

"I think that little fawn still had a few spots on him. Must've been late-born," Pop said.

"They didn't seem scared at all," Caitlyn replied.

Mom chimed in, "Well, I wonder if maybe they both figured if they kept real still, we wouldn't be able to see 'em."

"Talk about deer in the headlights. I don't think they knew what the heck we were," I laughed.

"Whatever the case, they was beautiful. Wish I'd had a camera," Caitlyn smiled.

"Wish I'd had a gun," Pop chided her.

Caitlyn took a large swipe at the water, drenching Pop with a splash. Shocked, he spun around in his inner tube splashing her right back. Mom couldn't let an assault on her only daughter go unanswered. So, she splashed Pop next. Then, came my turn splashing Mom. In moments, the serenity of the morning had exploded into a war zone of water fire, laughs, and screams of unfettered enjoyment echoing in every direction off the banks of the river.

When we settled on a particularly scenic gravel bar for lunch a couple hours later, I was reminded how famished doing absolutely nothing can make a person. In two sips, I drained one of the Mountain Dews that'd been chilling in the waterproof bag attached to Pop's tube. Mom hadn't made nothing fancy to eat, just white bread, Miracle Whip, bologna, and cheese sandwiches cut in halves from corner to corner. And there was potato salad, which was Pop's favorite, and Oreo cookies, which Caitlyn and me both loved 'cause they was store-bought, and we hardly never got store-bought desserts. In five minutes, all that was left of our feast were crumbs and swollen bellies ripe with contentment. I remember Pop telling Mom to stop her tidying up, and she did. He laid his head in her lap, she ran her fingers through his hair, and they both stared off at the Eden before them. Caitlyn moved over to a flat rock that jutted out over the water and lay down in the sun, eyes closed, lips pursed, straps of her swimsuit pulled down so they wouldn't leave tan lines. Me, I slipped back into the river and went completely under the water where there was no sound except the sizzle of oxygen bubbles as they escaped my cutoff jeans. When I came back up, I floated in place best I could, looking back at my family, smiling at the tableau of their repose, wishing it could always be this way, this freedom from all earthly disturbance—absolute bliss.

It was about two hours later, when all the peace that had pervaded the day vanished in a silent slipstream of water so deadly strong, it almost coulda gone unnoticed except it didn't. See, at one point the river widened out. Then, when the banks started to squeeze back together again, the current was suddenly accelerated real fast, sucking under everything it could and pushing it out far ahead. The scariest part is how it did this just under the surface without barely a whisper. In fact, in that wide part of the river, it was hard to know anything had even changed but for the temperature of the water that suddenly went ice cold and turned brackish. Mom was the only one to mention this phenomenon, and Pop followed up her surprised observation about the chill with some inappropriate joke about his balls, which made all of us laugh. Well, everyone except for Caitlyn, whose usual groan at such talk was all but expected. And I suppose that's why I looked around for her, only to see her inner tube empty, spinning wild in the water like it had been possessed by the devil. Instantly, a terror shot through me, and I yelled out to Mom and Pop, "Where's Caitlyn?"

The fear in my voice must've immediately struck a chord 'cause Mom and Pop both flipped around in their inner tubes, eyes darting every direction, panicked. Then, I saw it out of the corner of my eye, a tiny white hand accompanied a gargled cry as that hand was sucked under the surface of the water.

"Over there!" Pop yelled, and we both launched from our inner tubes swimming with every last ounce of strength we had to get to the last spot we'd seen Caitlyn. Of course, by the time we got there she was long gone. For her part, Mom was screaming her head off, doing everything she could to get some height from the perch of her inner tube where she hoped to spot my drowning sister.

I kept diving deeper and deeper into the water, flinging my arms every which way, hoping even though I couldn't see a damn thing, I might somehow touch a part of her. It was no use. The current was too strong. Every time I came back up to the surface, I was twenty feet away from the spot I'd just been. Pop's face was red and scared shitless, and he was practically unable to tread water himself, the current sucking at him too. And that's when it hit me, the best thing I could do would be to stop fighting, just hold my breath and sink. Maybe if I let the current take me, it would usher me along right to where Caitlyn was—to where I needed to be in order to save her. So, that's what I did. I stopped struggling against the invisible tentacles of suction wrapping themselves around my legs and waist. I let them envelop me in an icy embrace, and I disappeared into the depths of the river just like Caitlyn had.

As I was swept along that invisible undertow, I remember counting how long I'd been holding my breath, hoping that the same pull that'd sunk my body would soon spew me back up to the surface before all the oxygen in my being was spent. The relief I was waiting for did not come, though. My lungs pushed against my chest, demanding I find air, and my head went numb as I slid along under the water hoping against hope I would not crash into anything sharp. Then, just as I was prepared to charge up to the surface, I felt Caitlyn's hand limply flail into me. Fast as lightning, I grabbed it and jerked her lifeless body to me, swimming for the surface of the river with her tight in my arms.

Luckily, the shallows came up fast, and I churned through the water towards the nearest gravel bar where I let Caitlyn's body fall to the ground like a sack of cow feed. Closer than I expected, I heard Mom and Pop screaming, asking me if she was alright? But she was not alright. She was limp as a rag, the whites of her eyes peering at me like half-moons from behind half-closed eyelids. Her lips was purple and her skin was pale like the underside of a carp. I felt for a pulse, but there wasn't one that I could find. There was no life in her at all. Before I could think what I should do, Pop was rushing up next to me, pushing me out of the way, and compressing Caitlyn's chest with a force so violent, I felt sure he'd crack her right open. Then, he squeezed her nose tight and blew air into her body before pumping, once again. The next time he went to squeeze her nose is when her whole frame jolted in shock and water and vomit came spewing out of her all over Pop like a demon had been un-leashed from somewhere inside of her. As she gasped for air, she began sobbing, grabbing Pop like he was her life raft, and in fact, he was.

I'm not sure what anyone else really thought about that day, at least not deep down. We all breathed a sigh of relief, of course. And I guess the truth of the matter is, everything was fine. To me it was strange, though, 'cause after Caitlyn came back from the dead, after all the tears had been cried, and Caitlyn had cleaned herself off, after we'd all found our inner tubes and headed on down the river once more, we was mostly back to normal, talking and laughing and carrying on with our lives like nothing tragic had nearly happened at all. Was it really so simple as that? A family goes on a float trip. The current becomes too strong. A person dies. Then, they ain't dead no more. Everyone goes back to floating. Life goes on.

I'm not sure I said another word that afternoon, the image of the whites of my sister's eyes flashing across my mind ever more haunting with each bend of the river. She had been gone from this world total and complete—dead. I felt how cold she was, how lifeless. There was no spirit inside her flesh and bones anymore than there might be a spirit in the body of a stiff in some coffin. Then, there was life again, the whirring of the motors inside her sparked, veins and arteries jump-started to life. And now she was back. Her hair was once more in a bun on her head.

Her lips were pursed. She was adjusting her bathing suit straps so she didn't get no tan lines. And all I could think was there weren't no great mystery here. There weren't no grand maestro above directing our lives like his own personal symphony. There was only what was and what wasn't. The sun shines on water. The reflection of that sun off the water onto a surface, dances in a twirl of bright tendrils of light. Then, the sun moves on, and the light goes out. Ashes to ashes. Dust to dust. Alive yet inanimate. Fixed yet kinetic. Ephemeral yet permanent. Everywhere yet nowhere. Far as I'm concerned, this is the truth of our beginning and our end.

For some reason, I think there will be more significance to my last night milking the cows. Perhaps I hope somehow my interactions with Pop will be more meaningful too. In the end, though, the cows give their milk and eat their feed, and Pop and I clean up after 'em when they's through. My plan is to say goodbye in some way that later Pop can recall and know I was leaving this world in peace with him if nothing else. However, when the time comes to say farewell, it seems odd to do anything other than wish him goodnight. He nods back, though perhaps we do lock eyes a bit longer than usual, a bit more focused than usual. That's his way of letting me know he loves me, and my way of doing the same.

I'm still thinking about the depth of the look we exchanged on my way up to the house to collect the propane tank, when Mom steps out onto the front porch and motions to the grill parked nearby. "There it is. I was gonna get it ready for you, but them things is just too heavy for me nowadays," she says.

"Thanks again for lettin' me borrow this. I feel like an idiot forgettin' to pick one up in town."

Mom smiles, hugs herself. "It's gon' be cold tonight. Make sure you have some gloves and a good coat."

"I'm wearin' what I usually wear." I reach down to uncouple the propane from her BBQ. The tank is pretty near full, and she's right, it's heavy as all get up. I sigh as I lift it off the ground.

"What'd I tell you?" Mom asks, clearly seeing my strain.

"They makin' these tanks out of two-ton steel or somethin' nowadays?" I laugh.

"What your pop and me was talkin' about earlier..." she pauses, measuring her words, "You don't worry yourself none about that."

"I'm not," I say.

"I mean it. You and your pop is the exact same. He'll say he ain't worried about somethin', but really, it's eatin' him up inside. It ain't good for neither of y'all."

"Mom, it's alright," I assure her. "Really. I'm fine. You guys have done everything—*everything*—right by me, and you have to know that." I hope Mom won't read through my earnest sincerity and know something is, in fact, wrong.

Whether she can sense something off or not, I don't know. But she looks me square in the eyes in a way she ain't in a while, just like Pop did. "You promise me you'll hold your head up proud, now Calem. No matter what comes in this life, there ain't no reason for any of us in this family to feel ashamed. We ain't liars. We ain't cheats. We have always helped our neighbors and been there for one another. Maybe we ain't lived in a fancy house and ate caviar, but there ain't never been a time we was starved or left unsheltered. We have always figured things out, and we'll figure this out too." But suddenly, Mom's voice quivers and she shakes, a quiet sob breaking out from inside her, against her will.

Instantly, I run to Mom and grab her up in my arms, "Mom, it's okay. Everything's gon' be alright."

Mom shrugs off the comfort I'm trying to give and wipes her face with an old hanky from her pocket. "I'm sorry, Calem," she says. "I don't know where that came from. I'm just tired. Just plumb tired is all."

I rub her arm. It's the most consolation she'll let me give her. "I love you, you silly goose," I say.

Instantly, she laughs, "I ain't no goose. You know I hate you kids callin' me that."

"Well, when you's all honkin' and snortin' and carryin' on, what else are we supposed to call you?"

Mom laughs more and waves my words away with her hanky. "I *ain't* no goose."

"You'll always be my goose," I say, and I give her a smooch on the cheek. "I love you, Mom."

"Well, you have a couple extra hogsuckers for me tonight," she responds.

I know that's all I'm gonna get out of her, that's all she can give tonight. So, I say, "I will." Then, I grab the propane tank and head for my truck, letting Mom off the hook, assuring her as I go with my confident air, she ain't to blame for my troubles. There ain't a thing wrong with me with regards to her. No, sir. Not a one. Then, I throw the propane tank in the bed of my truck, hop in the cab, and take off down the road. And though the pain in my stomach wants to double me over, send me scrambling to some hospital somewhere, or worse to one of them crack houses in town where so many others have found ease from their pain, I refuse to let it. I'm too far down the path I'm on. I'm not turning back now.

When I get to my place, Miles is there waiting in his truck with the gigging boat hitched up behind it. Dixie is there too, sitting on the porch, tail thumping against the railing, wanting let inside where it will still be cold, but she knows I'll pour her a bowl of food. I park my truck, grab the propane tank from the bed, and meet both Dixie and Miles on the stoop.

"Thanks for grabbin' the gas," Miles says, taking the last pull on a cigarette before flicking the butt to the ground and stomping it with his boot.

"Oh, yeah. No problem," I say.

I lead our little caravan into the house. Dixie heads for her food bowl where I pour out a generous portion of dinner for her. Lord knows I want her to eat good tonight. I've heard of animals practically starving themselves to death when their owner dies, and I don't want that for her. Not that she really sees me as anything other than her gravy train.

Miles leans his overweight frame against the counter, removes a bright orange ski cap he's wearing, and scratches at his buzzed, brown hair. "It's gon' be colder than I thought. Maybe down near freezin' tonight. Still, my nads is hangin' about as low as they can go, seein' as I've got three layers on under here."

I head for the bathroom where I unzip and take a well-earned piss. I call back over my shoulder, "Can't be worse than last time."

Miles laughs, then coughs, "No shit. Last time was damn near hell. Weather's been strange this year, though. All over the place. Wouldn't be surprised if we get summer temperatures here in another week after this cold front passes."

"Maybe that climate change everybody's always goin' on about really *is* happenin'," I say, shaking myself off and zipping up again. I head for the coat closet where my insulated overalls hang.

"Oh, fuck no! Ain't no truth to that bullshit whatsoever. You know that. Just a bunch of crazy hippies yakkin' their traps," Miles says, and he fishes a box of cigarettes from his pocket. He wants one of his cancer sticks, but he knows I don't like him smoking in the house.

"Well, yeah. I know. But still, I sometimes wonder. Weather does seem to be gettin' weirder and weirder," I say. "And there's tornados all the time now. Remember that one touched down in Roby in the god-damned middle of February? That just wasn't right." I sit on the old couch in the living room to pull my overalls up over my boots and jeans.

"That's just nature. That's all it is. I've heard it's somethin' to do with the electromagnetic poles of the earth switchin' north and south," Miles says, and he coughs and puts his cigarettes back in his pocket.

"Electromagnetic poles?" I ask, as I zip up the front of my overalls and fish a ski cap out of one of the pockets to put on my head.

Miles nods, coughs again and snorts back some phlegm in his throat. "Yeah, it's true. The north and south poles is switchin' places."

"Why is the north and south poles switchin' places easier for you to believe than the idea we're just sendin' off too much shit into our own atmosphere?"

"'Cause it is."

"'Cause you read it on one of those whack job websites you go on?"

Miles clears his throat once more and sighs, annoyed. "At least I read. And what about you? You been talkin' to your sister?"

"It ain't like that," I say.

"It is, too, like that," Miles huffs. "Come on now. You know I hate it when your sister gets you all confused about things."

"I ain't confused. I'm just ponderin' out loud," I shoot back. "Since when can we not think out loud with each other? I mean look at us, we're dressed for the Arctic winter, and it ain't even November first yet."

Suddenly, my stomach is kicking me, so I grab a handful of antacid tablets and toss 'em in my mouth, crunching 'em up like little pieces of chalk. Miles sees this, and I know it bothers him how I eat antacids 'cause of my stomach pains. But what else am I supposed to do? I guess I coulda started smoking like him. Maybe that woulda been better. Too late now, I suppose.

"It's them polar vortexes switchin' places. I'm tellin' you," Miles reiterates.

"Go," I point Miles towards the door, as I turn off the lights.

"Texted Hatcher Mings," Miles says, as we step onto the porch, and I close the door behind us.

"He seem alright?" I grab the propane tank, and we head for Miles' truck. "Mom said Rhett was out of his coma."

"Yeah, he's woke up. But his brains is all scrambled. That's what Hatcher said."

I throw the propane tank into the bed of Miles' truck, and we load up into the cab. The inside of the truck is kinda like Miles' life—a mess. I have to kick empty bullet casings and a few crumpled Mountain Dew cans out of the way so there's room for my feet in the floorboard. Then, I grab an AR-15 leaning across the center console and set it in the half-cab behind me.

"Oh, give me that," Miles says. He takes the semi-automatic and rests it in the gun rack on the back of his truck window before jumping behind the wheel and starting up his truck, which has an obnoxious growl that could scare off wildlife ten counties away.

Despite the way he was raised, and how he kept everything so spick-and-span back in high school, it was after his split from Stacy that Miles let himself go. That was when he gained the hundred extra pounds and stopped caring if he smelled like the hardest working ashtray in the state. For the longest time, he stopped carrying himself like he did when we was kids, in that chest out, eyes bright, ignorance is bliss kinda way. I knew he was depressed, but then again, so am I. So is a lot of people. That's just kinda become part of our way of life around here. We's just learned to ignore our slowly dilapidating selves. As for Miles and me, we've continued on doing what we've always done: hunting, fishing, dating girls, getting drunk, and laying silly pipe dreams to nowhere.

As soon as we're out on the highway, Miles cracks his window and lights up. "Don't you wonder, though, if they don't tell us the truth about what's really goin' on?"

I realize he ain't given up on our earlier conversation about climate change. "They who?" I ask, as though I'm oblivious.

"The goddamned media."

"You really think they's all out there just makin' this shit up?"

Miles takes a long pull on his cigarette, coughs, "I ain't the only one questionin' it. There's lots of us who wonder what's actually real and what we've just been lead to believe is real."

I regret ever opening my damn trap. The mention of the environment is one of those triggers for Miles, like taxes and the Chinese. It makes him go off on crazy tangents and start talking all kinds of conspiracy theories. And Lord knows I *ain't* some environmentalist or nothing, but yes, I do wonder if maybe it ain't the craziest notion that somehow we's the ones causing all these God-awful weather conditions and whatnot. Well, not us here in the Midwest. Oh, hell no! I mean, the population of the entire state of Missouri is one quarter the population of a city like Los Angeles. I looked it up just to see if it was true. And honest to God, if there's anyone creating a problem for the environment, it's them, not us. Them, with all their stuff, and their stuff that needs stuff, and their stuff that needs stuff that needs stuff. Of course, they say we're the ones with the problem. Talk about bass-ackwards. I've seen the pictures of the plastic in the oceans along their coasts, all the pollution and runoff and the brown air and the mountainsides they cut into deeper and deeper to make their homes. It makes sense to me that humans is slowly destroying the only real free gift we've been given. That's what humans have got real good at, destroying the things they love. Still, places like LA is why guys like Miles don't want to admit there's a problem, and if there is, it ain't *his* problem. 'Cause, fact of the matter is, it ain't! When you's the only one living within five miles of another person, it's nature that'll come and eat you alive before the opposite happens. Still, we's the ones that supposed to pay for all the mistakes of those people living in those bloated cities. We's the one's who's supposed to be somehow responsible for everyone else's extravagance, just like me and my pop's little dairy farm is somehow responsible for the problems those big dairy operations make. And even though I raise a big ol' middle finger to anyone who can't understand the difference, I still never shoulda brought it up to Miles. And now I wonder whether I should just stay quiet for a while and then casually change the subject, or if me keeping my mouth shut will just create an opportunity for him to really go off? I decide to try staying quiet.

Thing is, Miles was always a mellow guy growing up, real sensible-like. He was the guy who'd make you pull over and pick up litter if there was some piece of plastic blowing around on the side of the highway. It was the divorce that set him back quite a bit, but it wasn't until that ol' reality star president came along that Miles was tweaked in just such a way that he became almost unrecognizable. Now, at first, it made me happy when Miles started talking about politics. I was glad he was gung-ho about anything at that point in his life. I mean, I don't know if the guy had even voted up until then. There was something about Trump and those rallies Miles went to that gave him a sense of belonging, made him feel proud of himself again. Next thing I know, he's flying an American flag on his front door and driving around town in his truck with big ol' MAGA signs on the sides. Trump was a hero to Miles, right up there with George Washington, Christopher Columbus, and well, Jesus Christ. All the things Trump represented spoke to Miles like nothing ever had. And hey, Trump spoke to all of us around here to a certain degree. I mean, we was already struggling, and suddenly, all these liberals are telling us we's supposed to let illegals take whatever jobs we got left. Well, Trump wasn't gonna have that. And we weren't racist, but we'd sure as shit seen towns burned down by Black folks just up the road in Ferguson, and you better believe that didn't win Black lives any favors from us. I could go on and on about the way Trump stood on our side of issues that was sensitive to us in a way no politician ever had. He made us feel powerful and understood 'cause he wasn't afraid of saying shit even if it was unpopular with the so-called intellectuals. What did he care? He didn't have nothing to lose. He was already a billionaire. So thankfully, he was our voice for one goddamned moment in time, and politically incorrect as he might have been, we loved every second of it—needed it, in fact.

Then, came the little breadcrumbs of doubt that perhaps ol' Don was a con, what with the money he seemed to owe to suspicious-seeming characters, the way he was all in love with Vladimir Putin, and the fact he was always promising us some spectacular trade deal with China, but it never seemed to materialize. And sure, Trump helped us dairy farmers out with that USMCA deal, but then he botched the whole Covid thing so badly, we was pouring out milk left and right. So, he ruined all the good favor he'd built up. Not to mention, it was a real drain, all the bellyaching and lying and, I don't know, irreverence that just poured out of him like sewage about women and colored folk and well, our military service members. For some of us who'd initially liked what he represented, we'd started to sour on him by the time he was booted from office. But for guys like Miles, his admiration of Trump was unwavering. Trump had given him permission to stand up for himself and what he believed in. He'd become just like Caitlyn, only the exact opposite. Then, there was the rest of us, stuck in the middle, flailing around like fucking idiots, knowing neither side was fully right, but also not knowing how to get either of them to see that. In the beginning, I tried to steer Miles away from the fringes best I could. In the end, I figured it was probably best to just look past it, all Miles' crazy talk about how Trump would rise again and next time him and his militia buddies was gonna make sure the election wasn't stolen even if that meant starting a war.

As we ease down to the river, we see a couple raccoons on the shore-line who stand up on their hind feet staring at us like we's part of some alien landing intruding on their otherwise normal evening.

"Them's a couple healthy-lookin' sows there," Miles says, and he begins backing the boat into the water. "Guess they must've found some fish heads somebody left or somethin'. They don't look too keen to take off."

"No sir, they don't."

"You wanna jump out and launch the boat?" Miles asks.

I exit the cab of the truck and head for the boat, release the trailer winch and safety chain. Then, I give her a little push back into the water. Before the boat gets too far from shore, I jump on in, start up the trolling motor, and leave it idling in place while Miles parks his truck and heads my way.

This particular area of the Big Piney where we put in is shallow but deep enough Miles' johnboat floats just fine. Miles churns through the water towards me and swings himself aboard with surprising ease considering his heft. I troll us out a little deeper, towards where cliffs the size of skyscrapers jut out of the water and shoot straight up to the night sky. I see a rope swing dangling from a tree that's somehow managed to cling to life on the side of one of these cliffs, and it reminds me of nights when Miles and me and a couple girls would come skinny dipping down here, climbing those rocks in nothing more than the skin God gave us, grabbing hold of whatever swinging rope was hanging around at that time and launching ourselves into the depths of the river below.

"Hit those lights, will ya?" Miles asks as he flicks on the lights mounted to the front of the boat.

I flick a couple switches on the lights mounted to the back of the boat, and suddenly, the world above us turns pitch black and the water below becomes clear as glass. Under those lights shining bright into the Big Piney, the colors beneath us appear so brilliant and alive, it's like you never seen 'em before. The river bottom sparkles like pirate's treasure, the gravel turning into rubies and diamonds and emeralds, streaked through with slivers of silver and gold. Moss and stonewort do other-worldly dances in the current next to coontails and watercress, swaying in time with tiny fish and even tinier minnows. Crawdads scoot backwards from boulder to boulder like they's being blown by some invisible wind while larger fish nestle in between velvety fallen logs to sleep through the night in peace.

"Look at that bass down there," Miles says, and he points towards a tangle of tree roots and logs draped in algae.

Sure enough, just beyond the willowy curtain of green, is a large-mouth bass, big as a cat, hovering solitary in the water.

"Old fucker," Miles says.

"Smart fucker," I smile.

As we get out into the river a little deeper, that's when we spot our first suckers. Their slim, grey bodies gently waver with the current down near the river floor.

"You see those guys down there?" I ask, and I slow the boat down to a gentle crawl just above where I spotted the school.

"I got 'em," Miles says. He reaches for one of the gigs on the side of the boat and balances himself up near the bow, holding up the gig with the four deadly spikes on one end like he's King Triton ready to do battle.

I do my best to keep the boat steady while I watch Miles gauge the depth of the river versus the refraction of its surface. He's damn near one of the best giggers I know 'cause of his ability to read the water proper, not to mention his ability to balance without falling overboard. And suddenly, almost faster than you can blink, he's jabbed the water with the gig and pulls it back out just as fast with a twitching hogsucker on the end.

"Look at that one! She's a beauty," Miles says. He flicks open a cooler and shakes the fish off into it. "First blood of the night!"

"Beginner's luck," I laugh.

"You wish, asshole," Miles smiles back.

Because Miles' gig dispersed the suckers, we'll have to troll around a little while until we find 'em again. Luckily, the wind ain't bad tonight, and no one else is out, so we got the river to ourselves, which is real nice. Nothing worse than another boat full of drunk yahoos carrying on and scaring all the fish away.

Miles lights up a cigarette. "I tell you they gave me a raise at work?" he asks.

"No sir, you did not. Congratulations."

"Thanks. It's just a couple bucks more an hour, but you know, every little bit helps."

"You sure they realized they was givin' that raise to *you*?" I joke.

Miles smiles wide, "Well now that you mention it..." And he busts up laughing, which is promptly followed by a hacking cough, and then another pull on his cigarette.

Somedays I wish I could be like Miles. Somehow, he moves through life like a cow chewing her cud. Sure things eat at him. That's why he smokes and drinks and eats too much. But I get a sort of comforting suspicion, he'll become an old man, still a little too large, puffing his cigarettes and laughing that laugh of his as he watches the sun go down on another country day. I suppose losing your parents is about the worst thing that can happen to a person. So, everything after that is tolerable. If there's anything I understand about Miles, it's how much he's been through, and my belly growls at me as I think about never hearing his laugh again or never being warmed by the sound of his smoke-filled voice. He's one crazy son of a bitch, but I suppose he's *my* son of a bitch. If the world was a little different—maybe if we was still boys—I'd wrap myself up in his arms and let him kiss my face, and we'd both understand for one single, solitary moment the absolute bliss of star-crossed lovers. But whether wrong or right, we remain the straight men we is, strong and solitary and ever standing at the doorway of a million different dimensions of ourselves, there's no way, at least in this life, we can ever otherwise know. We play our roles just like we's been raised to, just like everyone else around here.

Suddenly, my thoughts is interrupted by Miles.

"I've been thinkin' this summer we oughta drive up to Montana like we always talked about. I'd love to try and shoot me an elk or a bear. And hell, we should get out of this state at least once in our lives. What do you think?"

"That sounds real nice to me," I say.

"I'm serious," he says. "I think we should start plannin' it now, so we don't got no choice but to follow through."

"You should be keepin' your eyes peeled for fish is what you should be doin'," I respond.

"Yeah, yeah," he says. Then, he can't help saying more. "You know if we don't do it soon, we never will. That's what happens. You don't do somethin' and eventually the time passes for doin' it."

"I know," I say.

"Takin' chances. Ain't that what life's supposed to be all about?" Miles asks.

"I don't know that goin' on a trip to Montana is takin' some great chance."

"Then, I guess we got no reason not to plan it."

I don't want to talk about the future, about something that ain't never gonna happen. But I suspect the best way to shut Miles up about it is to just agree. "Alright, then," I say, resigned.

"You is just tryin' to get me to shut up," Miles huffs.

I don't admit he's right. I don't say anything. Best not to add gasoline to the fire.

Miles searches the water for suckers. "Little bit on up here to the right," he says.

I throttle down the trolling motor as we get to the spot where Miles indicated. Sure enough, I can see the same school we dispersed earlier. They're all congregating back together. "You got 'em?" I ask.

"Yup. I got 'em. Keep it steady." This water is a little deeper, and Miles takes an extra minute to read it before he readies his gig, and then—plop!—the gig slips into the water, and just as quickly slips back out with another fish speared clean through.

"That's a big one," I say.

"Yeah, well. At least now we won't have to share," Miles laughs, and he shakes the fish off into the cooler, which is slowly filling with slime, blood, and now, luckily, suckers.

I don't recall how exactly Miles and I end up next to a couple logs by the riverbank with a half-dozen hogsuckers filleted and turning into nuggets of gold in the fry cooker in front of us, but we do. The frigid cold is finally getting to me, numbing me, making me tired. And nearby the Night Call lurks, eager to creep in and scratch down the chalkboard walls of my mind with its splintered nails. The only way to hold it off is to stay awake and stay focused, just a little bit longer. *Calem, you can get through this,* I tell myself.

The boat is loaded up, the gigs are stowed away, and the propane tank that was the former bane of my existence now powers the flame under the fry cooker. As we wait for the batch of fish to finish cooking, Miles slices up onions real thin on an old cutting board and tosses 'em in the fish batter. "Will you grab those suckers?" he asks, a cigarette bobbing in his mouth. He motions with his fish-battered hands for me to pick up the deep-fry spoon, so I can scoop the cooked suckers out of the bubbling oil before they get too done.

The crusted curls of meat send off steam clouds and the aroma of sweet corn meal and spice into the night as I lay them out on a sheet pan covered in paper bags from the grocery store.

"Fuck, those smell good," Miles says, tossing the onions into the bubbling oil next.

I realize there's a six-pack of beer within arm's reach that's somehow been whittled down to only two. I reach over and grab the second to last can, pop it open, and take a sip. Then, I lean back against the log behind me. I watch Miles dab at the onions tumbling about in the fry cooker with the deep-fry spoon, making sure they get cooked evenly. There's a caveman-like quality to him squatted there on his haunches that makes me smile. This is the way humans have always been most fulfilled, sitting around a fire making food, I think.

"You oughta get married again," I say.

Miles looks over at me like I've just spoke French to him, "Why the hell would you say a thing like that?"

"Maybe it's the way you's tendin' to those onions, all nurturin' like," I smile.

"I ain't ever gettin' married again," he laughs, and he scoops out the onions from the hot oil and drops them onto the same paper covered sheet pan as the fish. More smoke. More aroma. Miles turns off the propane and pops the top on the last can of beer, leans back onto his own log to suck the rest of the nicotine from his cigarette before stubbing it out.

"You got any forks in that backpack of yours?" I ask.

Miles fishes around the backpack in which he keeps all his seasoning and cooking supplies. After a moment, he produces two forks and offers one to me. I take it and spear a small pile of fried onions right off the sheet pan. "I'm serious. You oughta do it. You oughta get married again," I say, once more, before taking a bite.

Miles don't answer. Instead, he picks up a hot piece of fish with his fingers and blows on it before throwing it in his mouth.

"It won't turn out like it did with Stacy," I say. "That was a real fluke. And it won't turn out like it did for your mom and pop neither, I promise you that."

"Come on, now. You can't promise me nothin'," Miles smirks. "That's just the truth of life. There ain't no promises."

"Well, still. There's an awful good chance it wouldn't turn out like last time. You're older now, and you know more than you did when you and Stacy got hitched."

"Uh-huh. Well, like I say, I don't want to get married again. I'm happy just how I am, thank you very much," Miles says. Then he snorts back some phlegm and pops another bite of fish into his mouth. "Fuck, I got a good do on this fish. Hits the spot, don't you think?"

"Yeah." But my reply must be a little too quiet or not enthusiastic enough. I see Miles squirm out of the corner of my eye, clearly uncomfortable.

"Why the heck are you suddenly carryin' on about me gettin' married?" Miles asks. "I ain't seen you on a date in almost a year." He slurps down more of his beer and belches.

"My situation is different," I say. "I work crazy hours all throughout the week and on the weekends too, and girls don't like that. You know how it is for me."

"Yeah, I know how it is for you." Miles scoops up a mouthful of onions with a roll of his eyes.

"What was that?"

"What?"

"That eye roll you just gave me."

Miles takes a moment from scarfing down food to breathe. He looks me square in the face. "Mandy."

"What about Mandy?"

"You ain't ever moved on from her," Miles states matter-of-factly. "When you move on from her, I'll move on from Stacy. Hell, we can double date and even have a double weddin' and everything. I'll pay for it."

"You're an asshole," I say.

"Let's talk about Montana," Miles replies without missin' a beat.

"Why are you so excited to talk about Montana all of a sudden?" I ask.

"I got that raise."

"And you just can't wait to blow it or what?"

"Maybe. It's the first time I'm gon' have a little extra cash since my divorce. Who cares? Don't you remember when we was kids how we'd talk about drivin' up to Montana, goin' all around the mountains and livin' off the land? There ain't no fences in Montana. Not like around here. Ain't no sales tax, neither"

"Let's talk about that some other time," I say.

"Well, you sure is in a mood tonight," Miles huffs. "Hardly said a word while we was giggin'. Then, you tell me out of the blue, I oughta go and get married. You upset 'cause I disagreed with you over the damn climate change situation?"

"No," I say, surprised that Miles has picked up on the fact I am indeed in a bit of a mood for reasons I will not be sharing with him.

Miles sighs, "Look, maybe you is right about climate change. I mean, you've always been way smarter than me. We both know that. It's just, you know how I hate all them idiots out there who think they's so much better than the rest of us. And sure as shit, you tell some liberal they's right about somethin' like climate change, and suddenly, they's wantin' you to pay for everybody's sex change operations and let colored folks tell you how you ain't good enough, like every single one of us hauled 'em over here from bumfuck Africa and at least half of us didn't fight for their fuckin' freedom!" Miles sighs again, nudges me with his foot. "I know you ain't some fuckin' liberal, and you know I realize it's probably all them cars and gas and exhaust and what-not that's causin' climate change. Probably all your fuckin' dairy cows too, by the way. There, you happy? Now can we talk about goin' up to Montana for real?"

As much as Miles might not want to talk about getting married again, I ain't gonna lead him on that I'm gonna in some way be around six months from now to go on a trip to Montana. So, instead of answering him, I say nothing.

"You alright?" he asks. "I thought you'd like the idea of finally doin' somethin' we've always talked about."

"I would." Then, I correct myself. "I do. I just...It's hard for me to commit to. That's why you need a wife, you know, someone to have around for when I'm not here."

Miles nods as if he understands or perhaps agrees with what I've said, but he don't clarify which part. Instead, he lights another goddamned cigarette and blows the smoke out into the night.

We sit there in silence for the longest time, neither of us touching what's left of the fish and onions still on the sheet pan, though it's mostly just scraps at this point. The only sound is the soft ripple of the river and the slight rustle of wind through the crusty dead leaves not ready to give up their perch on their trees just yet. Overhead, trillions of stars stretch out above us, each filled to the brim with wishes from ages past they ain't ever gonna make true. Not now.

Finally, Miles breaks the quiet calm. "We's all alone, you know. No matter who you are. Even if you got a sister or a brother or a husband or a wife or a mom or a pop, there's not a one of us that don't walk through this life completely by ourselves, if you really think about it. I 'spect I know this 'bout as good as anyone. All we ever really have besides ourselves is maybe a friend or two that sees the world same as we do, enough that maybe we feel like we're less alone than we really are once in a while. Thing is, you either fight it, or you embrace it. Me, I've learned to give it a big ol' bear hug."

I can't help but smile at Miles. "You're right about Mandy," I say. "I ain't ever gotten over her, even after all these years. I know I should. The world has moved on. We've both moved on. But I look back, and those were the happiest days of my life."

"Then maybe stop lookin' back," Miles says. "Maybe we's all gotta stop lookin' the fuck back."

I smirk. "This comin' from a guy who carries an AR-15 in his truck and prattles on about startin' a civil war 'cause he wants to make America *great* again."

Miles chuckles, "Oh, hell. You got me on that one. I won't even pretend you don't."

I look at Miles, and he meets my gaze steady as a rock.

"Let's plan that trip to Montana," he says again. This time he says it real soft and coaxing like I'd speak to a spooked heifer.

Suddenly, a tear drips down my face from where the fuck I don't know. I quickly turn and wipe it away. When I look back at Miles, he's still staring at me. He knows something is wrong, something big and deep that I ain't saying. Before he can ask me what it is, I stand. "We should get this mess cleaned up and head back," I say. And without waiting for Miles to respond, I get to work putting away our riverbank kitchen.

For a moment, Miles don't move a muscle. Then finally, he stubs out his cigarette and grabs the cutting board, knife, and utensils to go wash 'em off down in the river, while I uncouple the propane tank and check to make sure the fry cooker is cooled down enough I can strain the oil into an old Folger's tin Miles keeps handy.

Just about the time I'm hefting the cooker over to his truck, Miles reappears from the river with his utensils washed and put away in his backpack. He grabs the propane, and we secure everything in the bed of the truck so it won't roll around none. I wonder if Miles is gonna say something more to me, but I guess, according to my internal clock, it's 'bout midnight or so, and as such, we's both *way* past our bedtimes. I reach for my cell phone to see if I'm correct about the time, only to realize I left it in the seat of the truck. When I open the truck door and grab it, it blinks to life. Sure enough, it's about three minutes 'til twelve. But more importantly, there's about a half-dozen different voicemails and text messages from my mom staring at me. The last one is from only fifteen minutes ago.

Miles sees me staring at my phone perplexed, and he asks, "Everything good?"

I shrug and quickly go to my messages where Mom has left me five different texts asking me where I am, and why don't I have my phone on me, and to please call her. As I hit the number to call home, I motion for Miles to go ahead and get us on the road. "It's my mom," I say. "Somethin's up."

Miles nods, starts the truck and throws it into gear. And for what seems like forever, the line on the other end of the phone rings and rings and rings.

guess it's a self-sufficient Midwestern thing, the way we countryfolk handle problems. It's like it's best to keep it all close to the vest and not get anyone outside involved. Even the sheriff will be the first to try and get two sworn enemies to work things out between themselves around here, especially if they share blood. Back in the ol' days the only law around places like ours *was* family. Pop was the warden, Mom played guard, and everybody else did what those two authority figures told 'em to. There weren't nobody gonna come all the way out to the boondocks and enforce any other kinda rules anyway, especially on farms bigger than some counties. Even up to ten years ago, there was only dirt roads around here, and things like 9-1-1 didn't exist at all. I suppose that's why folks in the country is so keen on states' rights and keeping the government out of their business. That's the way we've been brought up, radical self-reliance. But this is also why things can get out of hand, how you end up with the horror stories about men killing their wives and burying 'em out in some cornfield or a woman starving her kids in some closet and nobody finds out until long after that wife is bone mill or them kids is dusty skeletons curled up behind storage boxes. It's a double-edged sword the freedom like what we got around here. On one hand, it allows you to make any decision you want for yourself. On the other, it don't stop you from making piss-poor decisions that can bring an end to life as you know it, right quick.

A couple years back, this exact dynamic played out with a guy and his wife who went by the last name Dotson. They lived a good ten miles away from Mom and Pop's place down a long dirt road. Nobody gave 'em much mind being as they seemed like decent people. They was real quiet and stayed out of everybody's hair. Well, little did we know, the

Dotsons didn't just believe in the end times, they was certain Gabriel had done blown his trumpet already, Jesus had returned, and we was all knee-deep in the tribulation period of the scripture wherein, according to prevailing belief, Satan gets to roam free of charge all over the earth. Well, apparently, the Dotsons was so certain of this, they had dug themselves a hole in the ground the size of a house and was living in it when we had an awful rainstorm and the whole damn thing caved in, burying them alive. County officials said what they'd done was about dumb as could be—building an underground bunker-like that without following any building codes—but who the hell was to know what they was up to given how far out here in the country they lived? Probably never would have found out about it neither, except they didn't pay their property taxes, and well, at some point the sheriff finally drove out to serve 'em legal notice. This crazy notion of rural freedom is what I'm thinking about as Miles and me fly down the highway in the middle of the night, me dialing home, racking my brain as to what the hell could possibly be going on.

I'm about to hang up on my third try calling Mom back when she finally answers. Her voice is strained, "Calem, why didn't you answer my calls?"

"Why haven't you answered mine?" I fire back.

"I've been out lookin' for your pop. He's gone off. And I don't know where he's gone to," Mom says.

"Pop?" I ask.

"That's what I just said," she huffs.

Why does this have to happen tonight, I think? Why tonight specifically does my old man have to go and cause trouble?

"He ate himself some dinner, and then he said he was goin' for a walk, and he ain't come back," Mom explains.

"He probably went over to that waterfall on Cantrell's place to see if them kids was gonna show up and try to cut through that fencin' we patched this mornin'."

"Well, he's got me worried," Mom says, and I can tell from the tone in her voice, she's pissed as hell too.

"What do you want me to do?" I ask.

"I want you to come over here and help me find him."

"Mom, he'll show back up. Just give him a little time. He ain't exactly had a stellar day. I suspect he might need a moment to himself."

"It's headin' towards one o'clock in the mornin'. How much more time am I supposed to give him? I mean, what if he's hurt himself, Calem? Remember that time he got his leg caught, and he was about to saw off his own foot just before you found him?"

Who could forget? I discovered Pop laying on the ground unable to move or free himself from a pile of logs that had tumbled over his left appendage. Though honestly, I still don't know if he was as certain about cutting off his foot as he'd claimed to be; it'd only been eight or nine hours.

"It's freezin' out there tonight," Mom pleads.

I look at Miles who can tell I ain't thrilled—not by a long-shot—about the conversation I'm currently engaged in. Then, I close my eyes and nod and hating the words about to come out of my mouth, I say, "Okay. I'll come over and help you look around, but I'm tellin' you he's gone down to that waterfall to make sure no trespassers cut through that new fence."

"Thank you, Calem. I'll put on some coffee and be ready when you get here," Mom says.

When I hang up the phone, I don't look at Miles. I don't see anything. I just feel more tired than ever, like I'm older than Methuselah and honestly, more ready than ever to fucking be done with this life. I'm also angry enough at my pop, I could scream. I'm pissed in a way I ain't been in a long time, maybe ever. It's so selfish what he's done, gone off and left Mom all worried, and me the one who has to show up, hunt him down, and play referee between them two. And for what, so he can scare off some kids who just want to enjoy that damn waterfall?

Ain't nobody gonna be down there tonight anyway. It's just like Mom said—too fucking cold!

"I'll come with you," Miles says.

"Naw, you don't need to waste your time," I assure him.

"I'm wide awake," he argues. "I had too much caffeine earlier. Besides, this is the most excitement I've had on a Saturday night in a while."

"It ain't Saturday night, not no more," I sigh, and I close my eyes again. I want to cry like a baby, but I can't—not right now. No, I gotta keep my shit together, and do one last good deed for everybody before I can take care of myself. Be the good son. Be the sweet brother. Be the best friend. Be everything you're supposed to be for everyone Calem Dewayne Honeycutt.

Just like he said he wouldn't, Miles don't turn towards my house. Instead, we drive on to Mom and Pop's together. Miles is giddy there's drama afoot he gets to participate in. And it's true, usually, there's so little going on even the smallest thing can get a person's blood flowing around here. I gotta admit, I, too, am now much more awake than I was twenty minutes ago, the frustrating turn of the night making me feel like I've just polished off a whole pot of Folgers.

I begin making a plan about what to do when we get to the farm. I wonder if Pop took his four-wheeler out to Cantrell's, and I wonder if Mom thought to check. I'm sure he did. It'd be a long walk all the way over there otherwise. Then again, if Pop was wanting to blow off some steam, walking a few miles in the dead of night ain't exactly *unlike* something he might do. That's the thing about my pop that makes him the kinda guy who can live in a place like we do and not just survive it himself but bring up a family here. He's strong. You think of the willpower it takes explorers to climb mountains and cross oceans and travel through space, and that's what it takes to start a farm, to work the land, to create the food thousands of folks rely on every day. When they begin recruiting to start a colony on Mars, they need look no further than a farmer who's worked below freezing temperatures in the winter and triple-digit temperatures in the summer without ever even thinking about shirking his duties. Farmers is *real* heroes, their skin crinkled from the sun, hands worn to the bone, eyes sharp as an eagle. Sometimes, I wish for just one day all the farmers of the world would go on strike, walk off their fields, away from their dairies, and out of their barns. Suddenly, all them city slickers who like to pretend us rural folk don't exist would know the anxiousness we feel all the time. They would realize right quick without us, they don't have shit for food and no way to get it neither. They sure as hell couldn't grow all the ingredients they need for all their fancy recipes, for all their crazy-ass diets, not in their little apartments. Maybe they'd give us the credit we deserve and the money too. Imagine if all the farmers rose up together—especially the little operations like my pop's—and they took back the reins from Big Ag and them yahoos who like to pretend milk and meat and fruit and vegetables all grow on aisles in some damn supermarket.

As for my pop, he's like me. It ain't in him to be anything other than a farmer. He wouldn't know what to do if he didn't have dirt under his nails and cowboy boots on his feet. Hell, even with cut-off shorts in the middle of summer, Pop would wear his cowboy boots. As kids, when my sister and me used to laugh at him for doing so, he'd tell us straight-faced his boots with shorts wasn't a fashion choice, it was just what was comfortable for him. As such, every summer, he took the farmer's tan to a whole new level. As for that dirt under his nails, Mom would beg him to keep his nails clean. According to her, it was just like shaving your face—the gentlemanly thing to do. After enough nagging, Pop would eventually perform what he called a "farmer's manicure." Watching the ten o'clock news, he'd pull out his pocketknife and go to town, scraping the undersides of his nails with the tip of the blade until they was white as daisy petals.

A lot of things about farmers is the same. Most folks ain't in farming for the money or the prestige, but there is this sense of pride knowing that you've put food on somebody's table, that you're able to take a tiny seed and a bit of earth or a baby calf and a little care and you's able to grow it into something useful the whole world over. And most of us farmers welcome the challenge of seeing if we can make a few extra pennies year over year by feeding just right or fertilizing just so. Do cows that listen to country music really produce more milk than cows that listen to classical? Who knows? But farmers will try anything once. It ain't glamorous, and Lord knows it ain't straight-forward, but somebody's gotta farm. So, we dedicate our lives to this thankless task, like unknown soldiers fighting the frontlines of an unspoken war, each season braving a new frontier of earthly and unearthly possibilities, both promising and potentially devastating. What other choice do we have?

When Miles slows down to turn onto the dirt road leading to Mom and Pop's, I realize he's been saying something to me about leaving the boat at my parents' house and us taking a shortcut to the waterfall by driving out to Highway 11, but none of this registers with me. And I'm about to ask him to repeat himself when I spot something out of the corner of my eye. Almost like a reflex, I stick my arm out and touch Miles on the shoulder.

"Stop," I say.

"What for?" he asks.

"Just stop," I bark. I blink my eyes and squint out the passenger side window of the truck, not sure if I'm seeing correctly.

Miles follows my gaze. "What is it, a deer?"

"There's a light," I whisper, "in the church."

Miles squints now too, looks out into the dark night at the small, country church that's barely visible in the front field of my folks' property. "I think you're right," he says.

It's the slightest glow, barely nothing, but it's there in the windows of the church nonetheless. Without a word, I open the door to the truck, get out, jump across the ditch separating the road from the pasture, and climb through the barbwire, heading for the church without a second thought. Even as I crunch through the frosted, dead grass breathing heavy against the icy night air, I can hear Miles calling after me, asking what the hell I'm doing, wondering if I want him to wait in the truck? I don't answer, because I don't know. Is that a light I see in the windows of the church, or is that the reflection of the moon? I can't tell. On crisp, cold nights like this the atmosphere is so clear and the moon gets so bright, it can play tricks on your mind.

In less time than I imagine, I'm at the stairs of the church and climbing up to the front doors, only to realize I don't have a key to let myself in. Still, I try for the door latch just in case. And, wouldn't you know, it's unlocked. As I'm about to open the door, however, I stop myself. If I indeed saw a light inside, that means people are inside, and depending on how many people there are—as well as their potential state of inebriation or drug-induced highs—I should be careful, I tell myself. Slowly, I squeeze the latch and open the door just a peek. With my eyes adjusted so thoroughly to the dark, the light inside the church that had seemed so dim now appears bright. It's a camping lantern set on the ground up near the altar, casting shadows up onto the walls and the ceiling in a ghoulish kinda way. Unable to see any activity to speak of, I open the door a bit further and stick my head into the sanctuary.

"Hello?" I call out softly.

There ain't no answer, just the creak of the wood as my weight shifts from one foot to the other, and I slip a bit further inside.

I raise my voice a bit more the second time, "Hello?"

Still no answer.

I look behind me wondering if I passed the owners of the lantern already, hiding somewhere out in the pasture, and I think if someone's broken in here, they's going to have not just me and my pop to deal with, but my mom also, especially if they gon' and messed anything up. That's when I remember, I'm actually supposed to be looking for my pop, right now. He's out somewhere in the woods, maybe lost, possibly hurt. And suddenly, I'm angry that I've been sidetracked by whatever wise guy has broke into someone else's house of goddamned worship.

"Hello?" I yell this time. "Whatever the fuck is goin' on, I ain't playin' around here!" I say, and I throw the door completely open and step fully into the church.

Still no answer.

"Fuck it," I whisper to myself, and I head for the front of the church. I'm taking that damn camping lantern of whoever broke in, and I'm leaving 'em in the dark. I'll deal with locking up later, after I find Pop and get Mom settled down. That's when I see him—a man sitting in the front pew, hunched over and praying, or perhaps crying. Instantly, I feel guilty for my anger, and I slow my march forward.

"Hello?" I say again. Suddenly, I question if this man is sitting there with a needle in his arm, high out of his fucking gourd, and I wonder if he's dangerous. Or maybe it's a woman. I can't tell.

"Can I help you?" I ask, almost reverently. I take a few more steps forward before the scene in front of me starts to become clearer. Even then, my mind has a hard time processing it. The person bowed in front of me don't look exactly like a person no more. They is all twisted and grotesque. There's black liquid sprayed out all around them. Some is still dripping onto the floor, and for whatever reason, I know there ain't no life in this form in front of me. There ain't no reason to tiptoe towards it, but I do. And then, it comes at me full force like a high-speed train, punching my insides with such ferocity, I double over and hit the floor, screaming out with a pain I ain't thought a person was capable of feeling. I hold myself on the floor like a baby crying for its mom, like a fucking wild rabbit caught in a trap. Then, I look up again unable to believe what my mind is telling me, what my body is being pummeled by—the truth: my pop is that grotesque form, that dead mass burst apart on that pew. I know that shotgun in his arms. I know those boots on his feet. That black goo everywhere is his blood, thick and ripe and spilt all over.

Suddenly, all the fish and onions I'd eaten with Miles comes spewing out of me with a convulsion of my muscles so strong I think it will crumble my ribs up and splinter my spine. And even after I'm empty of the acid in my stomach, my body still heaves determined to extract the poison that is surely killing me. But the toxin ain't something physical that can be released. It's mental, spiritual, other-dimensional, life colliding with death, expectation with reality, the worst kind of truth landing squarely in the center of one's mind. I squeeze my eyes tight and imagine some other place, some other time: Mandy and me making love in the back of my truck under the stars, talking to my cows while I stroke their teats and empty their udders, dog tongues lolling happily out the sides of their mouths, Mom frying food, Pop splashing me with water. Pop, the sun of my world, the gravity of my earth, angry, ol', stubborn, beautiful, sweet, wonderful Pop. He's alive, I tell myself. He's alive, and this is all just a dream. This is the Night Call. It's gotten me good this time! If I just open my eyes, nothing will be as it is in my head. I've let the Night Call run me through, but not if I open my eyes! So, I do. I open my eyes, but that form that used to be my pop is still there in front of me, even more real this time, even more lifeless and terrifying, disfigured like a hellish demon from a gunshot wound to his head. There is pieces of his brain on the pew next to him and running down the walls like human spaghetti. I look down and see that I'm knelt in Pop's blood and my own vomit, and I scream out in rage against another stab of pain to my belly. *Oh, Pop,* I think. *Why, Pop? Why?* And I reach my hands out to that monstrosity of flesh sitting on that pew, still holding that shotgun.

"Why, Pop?" This time I ask out loud, hot tears and snot rolling down my face. And I almost expect to get an answer. But I know the answer. I *have* known the answer for a while now. My Pop and I is exactly the same. We have touched the same joy and sadness. We have breathed the same hope and despair. We have known beauty and ugliness in ways no one can imagine. We was alone and together in this poor, stupid world of ours. I should have known the Night Call would get to him too. I should have known it would—*could*—wage war against both of us simultaneously, send its tentacles out to destroy more than just me, destroy everyone and everything, every tired and weary soul who ain't got much more than a hope and prayer, a Bible and a gun, maybe even less.

I crawl across the slime on the floor, like a toddler who don't know the first thing about walking, until I reach Pop's boot and pant leg and hands. I don't look for a face I know ain't gonna be there. Instead, I keep my eyes closed and rely on the sensations of my fingertips as I wrap my arms around him and hold him close to me. I see his smile. I see that mischievous twinkle in his eyes. I recall his laugh when he was playing a prank and that silent brooding glare he could give off when he was upset. I remember his smell like soap and milk rolled in flour and dust. And I cry. I don't even know where the tears come from. How is there so much water in me to make all these tears, all this snot and spittle that runs out of me from the tips of my toes and fingers and the recesses of my heart and mind?

As I hold Pop, I become aware of his shotgun at my fingertips, the sweet teat of death I have dreamed of sucking on for months now—maybe years—right at hand. Surely there is another bullet here in this place—peace and tranquility only a hairsbreadth away from me. Surely, I can join him here right quick. *Pop, I'm coming*, I think. *You can't leave me here alone, you son of a bitch. I'm coming too.* And I'm about to reach for that shotgun and check for that all too familiar sight of an unspent cartridge locked in its chamber, when I sense another presence and a hand on my shoulder, a human touch alive and real. For a moment, I think it's Pop. Then, I look back and find Miles squatted next to me, pale-faced and lost. He don't say a thing. He don't have to. I let go of my pop and cling to him, and he holds me and kisses my head like I'm his own child, and for a moment the burden of this existence seems lighter, light enough to take one more breath, to live one more minute. Only one more minute. Only one more breath. *Where is that gun*, I think to myself?

I thought I had faced death long ago. I believed I had stared deep into its eyes and embraced it full on. Not just my own. Not just my sister's. Growing up on a farm, death is everywhere, but I've learned there is a death you cannot be prepared for. It has no face and no body and no form to speak of. It is the silent, floating, mirage of life that exists forever just out of reach until one day it's gone. Whisked away like a shape in a cloud, this unexpected loss of a life you thought you possessed startles you like nothing else could, makes the ground beneath you crumble to dust, leaves you floating in a grey gulf of uncertainty like none you could've imagined. *Is anything real? Was anything ever?* One wouldn't think this new province of nothingness could lead to deeper revelation, yet it does. This absolute loss of gravity, of planet, of space, wipes clean a slate that once spelled out your existence with seeming clarity. Maybe all that you thought—all you believed up 'til now—has been an aberration too. Maybe the north and south poles *are* switching places right beneath our feet. Perhaps they are not just wreaking havoc in the depths of our celestial orb, not just changing the weather on its surface, but fracturing everything on earth, splitting apart the atoms of night and day, life and death, man and woman, old and young, black and white. The blind can now see. The deaf can now hear. The dumb can now understand. All of creation is born again, ushered to new life by the sound of sirens and screams and fragments of bone and flesh and blood and death. It's frighteningly cold too, this transformation. It smells of iron and piss and shit and bile. Then, I realize that smell is coming from me, has coated my legs and hands and arms and face like amniotic fluid on a newborn baby. But who will wipe it off of me? Who will scrape out the mucus from the inside of my throat? Who will cut the cord and help me breathe on my own?

The moon is still hovering overhead when I'm ushered outside the church by Miles, who cocoons me in his arms as though shielding me from death itself, or is it life he's fending off. Or maybe he's simply protecting me from the spinning bright lights of the emergency vehicles now parked along my parents' road, all strangely, eerily silent. This is not like Miles, to touch and hold, to coddle and whisper, but he does so with an ease that's welcomed by the parts of me still faintly attached to reality. As we cross the field now crystalline with frozen dew, paramedics move past us holding a yellow stretcher. They are going to collect their spoil, zip it up inside a sanitized black bag, and whisk it away like nothing ever happened here, like something worse than death don't exist. And suddenly, I hope Mom don't see it, the mess inside the church, the stump that was Pop. But she *has* seen it. I remember it now. She arrived after Miles but before the cops and the silent, rotating lights and the paramedics and their body bag. She is standing off to the side of the road talking to a highway patrolman with a bloated, stoic face. Mom is white as fresh cream, older than I've ever seen her, tear-stained but calm. There is blood on her too. *His* blood? There's a hole in the fence where someone cut through the three strands of barbwire once taut between two cedar posts in order to access the field. *They should have used the gate*, I think. *Pop will be so pissed.* Would *be pissed.*

Don't think the irony of this night is lost on me, the fact Pop beat me to the punch, stole my thunder, laid waste to my plans. His dead body could have been mine, my alive body could right now be his, though all the anguish would have still existed either way. I realize that. And perhaps now that I know I was not the only one in my family so haunted by the terror of our plight that I would take my life, I now must take more than my life. I must pick up my pop's heavy load as the only living survivor of us two. I thought he was stronger than me. I was sure of it. But no matter the case, he deserves the rest. He was clearly as weary as me, if not more.

I look up, and the slightest glow has pressed against the darkness of the sky, slowly elbowing it out of sight. A new day will soon be here. The fences will have to be patched up. Corn stover will have to be tilled down in the holler. Bills will have to be paid. Then, I remember...

"Miles," I whisper.

"Yes," he says.

"It's time to milk the cows."

"They'll be fine today," he assures me.

"No. We gotta milk 'em. Hurts 'em too much to leave all that cream in their udders. Don't matter what's happened. They gotta be taken care of."

Miles looks at the chaos around us. "Right now, though?" he asks.

"Right now," I say.

He nods, "I'll let the sheriff know you gotta get down to the barn. Is there anybody who can help you?"

That's when I realize probably nobody has called my sister and told her what's going on. I think of her because she knows how to milk cows. She knows how to herd 'em, disinfect their teats, and talk to 'em real nice. I fish my cell phone out of my pocket and find her number. I think when it rings that I probably won't get an answer, but right away, Caitlyn picks up.

"Hello?" she says. Her voice is high and sleepy. No one has told her about the evening's tragedy.

"Caitlyn," I say, my voice quivering more than I would like.

"Calem?" she asks. "It's four in the morning."

"Pop passed away, Caitlyn," I say. That's all I can manage to get out of my mouth.

There's silence on the other end of the line. Then, I hear a sharp cry like the last sound of a rabbit being killed by a coyote. I hear the rustle of sheets and Dan's voice, also sleepy, consoling Caitlyn, asking her what's going on.

"What happened?" she asks, suddenly back on the phone.

"He, uh...he shot himself," I say.

"Accidentally?"

"No. It weren't no accident."

"Oh my god!" I hear Caitlyn squeal again before her phone hits some hard surface and becomes garbled like the voice of a person talking underwater. The next wave of anguish begins to hit me again too, and I think I'm gonna pass out. So, I lean against Miles' truck. And I think again of that shotgun. *What happened to Pop's shotgun?* I wonder. Then, I scold myself for thinking such things, right now. How dare I? Mom is depending on me. Caitlyn is depending on me. Them cows is depending on me.

Suddenly, Caitlyn comes back on the line. "Where's Mom? Is she okay?"

"Yeah, she's right here," I say. Then, I keep going. "You should probably come home. The cows—they need milkin', and I think there's trouble here on the farm. I think we's plumb out of money."

"Is that why Pop shot himself?" Caitlyn asks, barely able to get the words out of her mouth.

"I think that's part of it," I say.

"How can y'all be out of money?" Caitlyn asks.

"Things ain't good. I told you that earlier when we was talkin'."

"You didn't tell me nothing like that!" she suddenly yells.

"Well, I'm tellin' you now, then," I say. "There's real problems down here. The co-op is kickin' us to the curb, and the cows —"

But suddenly, I'm interrupted by Caitlyn, "Fuck the cows!"

"No, you can't just say fuck the cows," I counter. "We got obligations to them heifers—*especially* to them heifers. We can't just let them stand around with their udders full."

"You can too!" Caitlyn says. "Fuck the cows! And fuck the co-op! Dad's dead! And fuck you for even thinking about anything other than that right now!"

"Well, I'm sorry," I say, "But don't you understand what's goin' on? We's in a bind. Don't matter if Pops dead. We got obligations, and part of the reason I'm callin' right now is 'cause I need you. I can't ask Mom to help me at the barn, not with the state she's in. And I can't afford to hire anyone to help me, not that there's anybody left around here who knows anythin' about dairyin' anyways. I need you to come down here, and —"

"And what, milk cows with you?" she laughs, deliriously. "I am not coming home to milk those goddamn cows and to work that fucking farm. Lemme talk to Mom!"

"Mom's talkin' to the highway patrol right now. They's takin' her statement. But look, she ain't in a good way," I say.

Suddenly, I hear more static on the other end of the line—clicks and shuffles and thumps. Then, Dan comes onto the phone. "Your dad passed away?" he sort of half-asks, 'cause he's clearly got the gist of my conversation with Caitlyn.

"Yeah," I say quietly.

"Look, Caitlyn's real upset, right now. I'm gonna get her calmed down, and then we'll figure out what we're gonna do. We've got the kids to think about here and work. We can't just drop everything and come down there right this instant."

"I know you've got obligations. I'm just tellin' y'all, we could use you down here as soon as possible. There's a lot goin' on."

"You need me to wire you some money?"

"No. That's not what I'm askin' for," I hear myself almost yell out.

Dan is silent, and I'm pissed as hell. Yes, there's money problems. There's all kinds of fucking problems. One of the biggest problems is that Caitlyn has always claimed to have all the answers, and now that we need her help, she ain't available. But then the truth is, she ain't ever been available. She hightailed it outta this place the moment she was old enough, and now I'm alone, and I can't do this all alone. *I just fucking can't!*

"We'll get back to you real soon," Dan says, and he hangs up the phone.

For a moment, I'm stunned by the silence on the other end of the line. But it's more than silence, it's a total misunderstanding of our plight. Do I want to mourn my pop? You bet your ass I do. But we have a farm to run. We have cows to take care of. A check ain't gonna help that—not this morning, not right now! We need more than that; we need help! *Real* help! *Come on!* I wanna scream. *Fuck!*

I realize my eyes is clenched shut, and I'm squeezing my phone so tight with my hand I might crush it when Miles touches my shoulder gently. He's returned from talking to the sheriff or the highway patrol or—I don't know—someone in charge. "It's gon' be okay," he says. "What do you need me to do?"

I look around for Mom, but she's crossed the ditch and is headed for the paramedics who are carrying that yellow stretcher and what's left of my pop now zipped up like meat scraps in a garbage bag. She's wailing out. I can hear her howl like a bobcat in the night. It's something she don't know how to do—scream in pain. She's never vocalized pain or made a show of her emotions, especially in front of strangers. But suddenly, there she is. She starts to hit the paramedics, shoving them, trying to get them to let go of that body bag of theirs, to give it to her. She'll take it back to the house and fix it up. That's what she does. She takes two pennies and rubs 'em together and makes a fucking life. At this point, she's like a starving animal. She'll eat the scraps, don't matter what they are. Before she can knock any of them boys off their balance, the sheriff is there—or maybe it's one of his deputies. He holds her back, squeezes her arms with his hands so tight I know he'll leave bruises on her soft, clay skin.

I want to go to her, to console her. But she don't want me. She wants my pop. That's all she ever wanted in this life, and now he's gone. So, I turn to Miles who is waiting ever patiently for whatever command I might give him. "We gotta get down to the barn. We gotta bring up them heifers," I say.

He looks at me, then out at my mom who has melted into a heap at the sheriff's feet, watching solemnly now as the paramedics continue their procession and load Pop's pieces into the back of the ambulance to haul them away.

"What about your momma?" Miles asks.

"She'll either freeze out here or grab her cleanin' supplies and start cleanin' up that church." Either way, I know my mom don't want to be touched. She don't want to be reasoned with. Silly goose. All she wishes she was doing was making a fresh pot of coffee for me and Pop to drink before milking or clipping coupons in the house to trade with the other ladies in town, anything but being *that woman* who needs something from us—from men who have never understood her, who have only ever seen her as a means to an end. She is the garden that has given for no reason other than that's what's been expected of her. The tastiest morsels of her existence have been devoured by us with little thought or appreciation. All she hoped for in return was to exist in peace under the sun, but now she will grow wild without nurture until the weeds overtake her, until she returns to the dust from which she once rose with so much promise and so much pride.

The girls have already made their way up to the milk barn without any of the gentle encouragement they're used to. They wait in line at the gate to the milking stage wanting us to relieve their udders. Miles and I let Bert in first like usual. She's followed by Mandy and all the others, same order as any other day. They don't know about the terrors of the world just outside this barn. They eat their food and give their milk and wait to be told what else to do.

Miles helped out enough around the barn when we was younger, he's not exactly a stranger to the equipment and the process, and for some reason, he's still here, right next to me. He just needs a little refresh. Push that button. Check that pressure. Open that gate. I wouldn't usually let him smoke in the barn, but today is an exception. Today, I love him for the cigarette bobbing up and down in his dried, thin lips and the bloodshot blue eyes with which he watches what he's doing so careful. He is all I have now in my hour of need. Perhaps he is *all* I have total and complete. Not my mother. Not my sister. Not my father. Even the Night Call seems to have abandoned me with its whispers so sordid and self-righteous. Perhaps this is because I've been birthed anew to this world in some odd way. Death—not mine—has given me hope. I'm looking at it, turning it over in my hands, considering the loose fragments of it like glitter in a snow globe drifting into a new revelation before me. Gone is the guilt of not being enough for everyone else. Shoved out of existence is the careful consideration of opinions and thoughts formed far away from this place. *Miles*, I want to scream. *Miles, I understand now!*

Suddenly, ideas dance through my mind challenging what is right and what is wrong, twisting and turning and jumping and throwing their heads back, laughing in blissful ignorance. Fact and fiction become funhouse mirrors instead of a straight-edged torture I have brought on myself. Why should the world be seen through one person's lens and not another's? I have lived by someone else's code of morality and that has brought me to the brink of the grave and destroyed my pop complete. But why live by it anymore? Why survive by highfalutin ethics that don't include you? It is taxation without representation! I am a straight, white man who extracts the milk from cows' teats to feed thousands, yet I am starved both in my body and mind, held prisoner by a worthless shame hung 'round my neck. I shoot guns and gig fish, and I live in a house made of my blood and bone, yet this way of life is considered trash to the hoards beyond the green of my forests and fields. I follow the first commandment ever given. I have taken dominion over the fish of the seas and the fowl of the air and every living creature that crawls upon it. The ground I stand upon is all I've ever known and all I'll probably ever know. Perhaps a new beginning lies here in this new understanding.

I look at Miles, and I see something I ain't ever seen before—more than a friend, more than a brother—a partner in survival as we face an army that's surrounded our little Eden and chomps at the bit to swallow us whole. Caitlyn is not here. All those who say they know better ain't here. Miles is here. He is in the shit with me, wading through the manure and blood and bile, cigarette in his mouth. And suddenly, I understand his railing against the system these last few years, his hate of those people out there who think they know us, but they don't. They have no clue, and he's right. They don't just eat the food we grow without an ounce of gratitude for it, they feed on our souls too. They've convinced us their way is the only way, and if we step out of line, we is condemned to their eternal disdain. This is hell in its own right. I see this suddenly so clear, it's like shining a light in a dark river.

I think of the shotgun in my pop's cold hands, and then I think of my own. Why turn our guns on ourselves overwhelmed by our inability to measure up to the impossible standards set for us, standards that never included us in the first place? Why fall prey to vampire souls who suck the marrow from our own and then mock us for rotting on the vine? This is what Miles has been trying to tell me. This is what all those others draped with red, white, blue, and the anger of radicalization have been screaming about from their pick-ups and hot rods and cornfields and dairy farms and churches and graves—all them folks I had once thought of as unhinged, untethered, deplorable. But now I know I have joined their chorus. It's the only way to survive the Night Call, I now realize that—like the very sun coming up outside.

Scream louder than the Night Call—overwhelm that stupid guilt from a church you ain't a member of, that religion of what's popular and acceptable and supposedly moral and decent. If dying off slowly or flat out killing oneself is what is moral and decent, I choose to redefine decency and morality under terms in which I don't have to wither away. How about I tell you out there what is acceptable for once? After all, I am the one who gives you the sustenance of your very life. I give you the milk that your mother no longer can! I have a shotgun *and* a rifle, and I am a good fucking aim!

I scream in my mind at my sister and all those like her. I scream at the bankers and the politicians and the big businesses and all their PC bullshit. They are the Night Call. They are the ones who have crept into my bedroom and laid waste to my existence, but not just my existence, my pop's—my sweet, beautiful, wonderful, stupid, stubborn pop! But why let them? *No! Not anymore.* I choose to still the Night Call. I choose to sleep peacefully. I choose life for myself even if that means rising up. Why not turn all my will and my rage outward to those who rape my people and pillage my land and then laugh at me for crying? Am I calling for civil war? I am calling for a war to recognize *my* birthright. *Mine!* Just like everyone else, I matter! *I must matter too!*—a middle-aged, straight, white man with nothing to my name but a gun and a prayer. Wash away my guilt and my shame. I am who I am. Maybe I am nothing more, but I am certainly nothing less. Shine the light in the dark for us less than, us poor scum, us stupid idiots with hungry bellies gutted by folks who have no right to see us as such. *Still the Night Call,* I yell out to anyone who will listen! *Still the Night Call...for the sake of all of us!*

REFERENCES

Baurer, Kathleen. (January 3, 2018). *'Big Milk' Brings Big Issues for Local Communities.* https://civileats.com/2018/01/03/big-milk-brings-big-issues-for-local-communities/

Calamur, Krishnedev. (June 11, 2018) *Trump's Beef With Canadian Milk.* https://www.theatlantic.com/international/archive/2018/06/trump-canada-dairy/562508/

Estabrook, Barry. (August 10, 2010). *A Tale of Two Dairy Farms.* https://www.theatlantic.com/health/archive/2010/08/a-tale-of-two-dairy-farms/61192/

Gowen, Annie. (December 26, 2019). *In Trump Country, A Season of Need on Family Farms.* https://www.washingtonpost.com/national/in-trump-country-a-season-of-need-on-family-farms/2019/12/26/fcb71262-2377-11ea-86f3-3b5019d451db_story.html

Gowen, Annie. (November 9, 2019). *I'm Gonna Lose Everything: A farm family struggles to recover after rising debt pushes a husband to suicide.* https://www.washingtonpost.com/nation/2019/11/09/im-gonna-lose-everything/?arc404=true&itid=lk_readmore_manual_50

Kaufman, Dan. (August 10, 2020). *Letter from Wisconsin: How Suffering Farmers May Determine Trump's Fate.* https://www.newyorker.com/magazine/2020/08/17/how-suffering-farmers-may-determine-trumps-fate

Kral, Linni. (August 22, 2017). *The Fight for America's Disappearing Ancient Dairy Cows.* https://www.theatlantic.com/science/archive/2017/08/america-heritage-cows/537507/

Kurlansky, Mark. (2014). *Inside the Milk Machine: How Modern Dairy Works.* https://modernfarmer.com/2014/03/real-talk-milk/

Lowe, Peggy & Morris, Frank. (January 8, 2020). *Floods, Bankruptcies, Trade Wars, and Politics — What Agriculture Means for Kansas City in 2020.* https://www.kcur.org/agriculture/2020-01-08/floods-bankruptcies-trade-wars-and-politics-what-agriculture-means-for-kansas-city-in-2020

Nightingale, Joseph. (2020). *Why Don't Conservatives Believe in Climate Change.* https://medium.com/bigpicturenews/why-dont-conservatives-believe-in-climate-change-157299cd6f1e

Pitman, Lynn. (December 2018). *History of Cooperatives in the United States: An Overview.* https://resources.uwcc.wisc.edu/History_of_Cooperatives.pdf

Pollan, Michael. (2016). *Big Food Strikes Back: Why did the Obamas fail to take on Cooperate Agriculture?* https://www.nytimes.com/interactive/2016/10/09/magazine/obama-administration-big-food-policy.html

Reed, Elodie (October 11, 2018) *The Cow-Milking Robots Keeping Small Farms in Business.* https://www.theatlantic.com/business/archive/2018/10/young-dairy-farmers/567937/

Roman-Alcalá, Antonio. Montenegro de Wit, Maywa. Liebman, Alex. Chrisman, Siena. (February 2018). *The Agrarian Origins of Authoritarian Rural Populism in the United States: What can we learn from 20th century struggles in California and the Midwest?* https://www.researchgate.net/publication/322869421_The_agrarian_origins_of_authoritarian_rural_populism_in_the_United_States_What_can_we_learn_from_20th_century_struggles_in_California_and_the_Midwest

Siegel, Rachel. (January 6, 2020). *Borden Dairy becomes second major milk producer to file for bankruptcy in two months.* https://www.washingtonpost.com/business/2020/01/06/borden-dairy-files-bankruptcy-amid-debt-load-headwinds-facing-milk-producers/

Simmons, Dan. (January 18, 2020). *Fighting Suicides in Dairy Country Through 'Farmer Angels'.* https://www.washingtonpost.com/national/fighting-suicides-in-dairy-country-through-a-farmer-angel-network/2020/01/17/33f3f584-38c6-11ea-9541-9107303481a4_story.html

Van Dam, Andrew & Karklis, Laris. (December 30, 2019). *With Trump's Farm Bailout Came Surprising Profits, but Little Help for the Neediest.* https://www.washingtonpost.com/business/2019/12/21/after-miserable-farm-sector-still-came-out-ahead-thanks-government-assistance/?arc404=true&itid=lk_readmore_manual_52

Whites-Koditschek, Sarah. (February 28, 2019). *Most Nitrate, Coliform in Kewaunee County Wells Tied to Animal Waste.* https://www.wisconsinwatch.org/2019/02/most-nitrate-coliform-in-kewaunee-county-wells-tied-to-animal-waste/

(September 30, 2020). Top 10 Poorest States in the U.S. *https://www.fcnl.org/updates/top-10-poorest-states-in-the-u-s-1630*

Cooperatives — An Overview. https://nationalaglawcenter.org/overview/cooperatives/

Fish Gigging. https://huntfish.mdc.mo.gov/fishing/get-started-fishing/fish-gigging

How Milk Gets from the Cow to the Store. https://milk.procon.org/how-milk-gets-from-the-cow-to-the-store/

List of Missouri native plants. https://en.wikipedia.org/wiki/List_of_Missouri_native_plants

Poverty Facts: The Population of Poverty USA. https://www.povertyusa.org/facts

CPSIA information can be obtained
at www.ICGtesting.com
Printed in the USA
LVHW092032291221
707463LV00010B/152/J